BIG
WATER

BIG WATER

Andrea Curtis

ORCA BOOK PUBLISHERS

Library and Archives Canada Cataloguing in Publication

Curtis, Andrea, author
Big water / Andrea Curtis.

Issued in print and electronic formats.
ISBN 978-1-4598-1571-1 (softcover).—ISBN 978-1-4598-1572-8 (pdf).—
ISBN 978-1-4598-1573-5 (epub)

I. Title.

PS8605.U777B54 2018   jc813'.6   C2017-904534-2
C2017-904535-0

First Published in the United States, 2018
Library of Congress Control Number: 2017949697

ONTARIO ARTS COUNCIL
CONSEIL DES ARTS DE L'ONTARIO
an Ontario government agency
un organisme du gouvernement de l'Ontario

Summary: In this historical fiction for teens, Christina and Daniel struggle to survive when the steamship *Asia* goes down in a violent storm.

RECYCLED
Paper made from
recycled material
FSC® C103567

Orca Book Publishers is dedicated to preserving the environment and has printed this book on Forest Stewardship Council® certified paper.

Orca Book Publishers gratefully acknowledges the support for its publishing programs provided by the following agencies: the Government of Canada through the Canada Book Fund and the Canada Council for the Arts, and the Province of British Columbia through the BC Arts Council and the Book Publishing Tax Credit.

Cover illustration by Jacqui Oakley
Edited by Tanya Trafford
Design by Rachel Page
Author photo by Joanna Haughton

ORCA BOOK PUBLISHERS
www.orcabook.com

Printed and bound in Canada.

21 20 19 18 • 4 3 2 1

For Flo

On September 14, 1882, the steamship Asia sank in a violent storm on Georgian Bay, killing some 140 passengers and crew. It is considered one of the worst disasters in Great Lakes history. The only survivors were two teenagers.

One

The wind blasts my face. It's hard, like pebbles kicked up behind a wagon taking off at full tilt. It hurts a bit, but it's also satisfying. Bracing. Like I'm facing my fate head on. I know that sounds romantic. Or maybe just silly. But after everything I've been through, don't I have the right to be dramatic?

What I should be, really, is frightened. Everything about this situation is alarming. I can almost hear the opening strains of one of those melancholy operas Father likes to listen to with the door to his study closed. All the ominous parts are here—dark sky, turbulent lake, waves rising, my cousin Peter, the ship's first mate though he's barely older than me, insisting I get a life preserver and put it on.

I dig my nose into my collar and turn to the side. The wind still tears at my skin, but I'm not going to leave this spot at the front of the ship if I can help it. Even though the sky is getting darker by the second. Even though it's only midmorning, and I can barely see the horizon. The lake is murky too, almost black, indistinguishable from the sky. At least here I don't have to listen to the others. At least here I can be alone.

I can see the animals are restless, tied up on the nearby deck. Chained to the ship and each other, they have no choice but to face their fate. The horses are wild-eyed, ears pointy. One nips the other in the neck. The mare kicks her hind legs at the bite, and it sets off a chain reaction, like when someone cuts in line at the bank or the church Christmas bazaar, and everyone is outraged.

That definitely sounds silly, comparing frightened horses to old people at the bank or buying shortbreads and sour-cherry jelly. I know nothing here is funny. It isn't silly. But ever since Jonathan died, I find it more difficult than ever to react properly. The worst was when I had a laughing fit at the funeral. I tried to disguise it as sobs, but Mother knew. So did Ally. She always knows.

I should go right now to the spot under the stairs where they keep the life preservers. I know I should. Peter sounded serious. And he knows the lake. He's been working on the water since he was twelve. He's been through more storms than I can count, even a wreck or two.

But I've spent too much time on Georgian Bay to put too much weight on warnings in the sky or even the shouts of harried crewmen. The weather comes and goes like the hourly train. You don't like it? Wait a minute and it'll change. Just as soon as you think you know what's what, the barometer goes up, it goes down, thunder rolls through with hardly a drop of rain. I've heard those old sailors who hang around the dock at Owen Sound say they have a weather eye. They claim to read the future in the patterns of the clouds, the color of the sunset or sunrise. But as far as I can see, they're wrong as often as right.

Anyway, it's hard to know where a sailor's worry ends and a cousin's anger begins. Peter was furious when I turned up unannounced at the dock in Owen Sound last night. He nearly lost his top when I told him I was running away from home. He said it was his duty to inform Captain Savage, and that he himself would tear up my ticket to Sault Ste. Marie. I could practically read his mind: *As if I don't have enough to do without Christina to watch out for.*

But I don't need a chaperone. I'm practically a grown woman, for goodness' sake. Seventeen just last week. My first birthday without Jonathan to share it. But Mother and Father have barely noticed that I don't need someone holding my hand. Mother speaks to me as if I'm a fool or an imbecile, as if I need to be told how to behave. As if it's her job to map my life out for me. Isn't that the thing about growing up? You get to live your own life. Make your own decisions.

Mother and Father apparently have other ideas. I left before they had a chance to send me away, to farm me out to be a nursemaid or country teacher or worse. They think I don't know they want to be rid of me. Mother doesn't say it. Not in words anyway. But I see that expectant look flicker across her face when she hears someone at the door, and the pained, disappointed expression when it's me instead of Jonathan who comes into the room. I know she's lost patience with my wandering and my dark moods. I even see her grimace when I smile, a smile everyone says is exactly the same as his. She can't stand the sight of my face. It's a reminder of all that she's lost.

Frankly, I'm still not sure why Peter didn't do as he threatened and kick me off the steamer or have the constabulary take me home. Maybe he could see the determination I'd first arranged on my face when I walked out the door of our house and over to the train station in Parkdale. I refused to look anyone in the eye—not the barrow boy or the newspaper agent I've known all my life, not the milkman or any of the delivery men with their wagons piled high. On Queen Street, I even passed our old Sunday schoolteacher and the kind neighbor with her new baby in a pram. I ignored them all, picking up my skirt to keep it out of the mud. I didn't look anywhere but straight ahead until I got on the train and collapsed in a heap.

Or maybe Peter just felt sorry for me. I promised him I'd let my parents know I'm fine once I've put the lake and several hundred miles between us. I told him I needed to get away. The Soo first, then who knows? Maybe just for now. Maybe forever.

A wave splashes over the deck, and I have to lift my feet to keep my boots dry. I can see the whitecaps now. The waves are growing bigger, their furious tops glowing white against the gray. The bow pitches down low, and I have to grip the guardrail to keep from falling forward. The wave is so deep, the water is right beside me. So close it looks as if it's going to fall over top of me like a heavy velvet curtain. I take a deep breath and squeeze my eyes shut.

But the wave passes. The boat emerges. I open my eyes. My hair is wet, my boots sopping now. The horses are making a racket, neighing and whinnying. The cows have gotten into the act too. They're making such an unholy noise, I'm going to have to find another place to face my fate.

More people have arrived on the upper deck, negotiating the cargo strapped here—barrels and stacks of goods wrapped in canvas, a few red-hulled rowboats, a canoe leaning up against the rail, some luggage too. There's a businessman in a fine suit and hat who's striding around like he thinks he's in charge. He bellows at a trio of rough-looking lumbermen headed up to the camps, but his voice is lost in the wind. Or maybe they're ignoring him. All three are talking at once, growing more animated with every word. Two crewmen rush by, cabin boys barely out of short pants, going in and out of doors, doing who knows what. I feel invisible here, as if I am watching it all from the other side of glass. I am removed. Apart.

A young mother with her small child comes up to the railing behind me, the boy's legs wrapped tightly around her waist, arms circling her neck. The woman looks as frightened as the horses. I stare at her faded canvas-colored life preserver, wondering what she's heard. I'm about to ask her, to break through the invisible glass that divides me from the rest of the passengers, when the child throws up all down her back.

I gulp and turn away. I've never been one of those people who can help sick people. I can't imagine why Mother would think I'd be a good governess or nursemaid for anyone. There was this girl I used to play with when we were small who was always nursing small animals back to health and insisting on playing doctor and patient. She tried to get me to go along with it, tried to get me to make bandages and poultices for dolls and the smaller children on our street, but I could never participate in the way she wanted. I didn't show adequate enthusiasm for her caregiving games, and she eventually moved on to other girls. It's not that I don't care about other people. I'm not cruel, not selfish, no matter what Mother says. But I just can't seem to be helpful. It was the same when Jonathan was sick. Seeing that child throw up all over his mother just makes me want to throw up too.

I hold the railing tightly as I move sternward along the promenade deck that encircles the boat. My boots slide on the slippery surface. All but one of the oil lamps that swing from the walls along the walkway have gone out.

The *Asia* is a tall ship, taller than most of the steamers I've seen at dock in Collingwood or Owen Sound. Even here at midship I'm high above the waterline. She's a riverboat, Peter told me, built tall to fit through narrow canals.

Without warning, the *Asia* pitches to the side, and I lose my balance, falling into a door that opens with my weight. An old woman, her gray hair loose and stringy around her shoulders, screams and pulls a blanket up to her neck. There's another, much-younger woman on the double berth down low, and she looks at me with saucer eyes.

"Sorry!" I mumble and scramble to my feet, trying to get out as quickly as possible. The room is nearly as small as the bedroom closet at our house in the city. The woman with the long hair reminds me of a ghoul, her face hollow and gray. I grab the doorframe and hoist myself upright. The boat lurches the other way, and I stagger onto the deck, the door slamming closed behind me. I see more people coming out of rooms, holding their stomachs, racing to the side to lose their breakfast overboard.

I've got to find my cousin. Ask him where I can stay out of the way of all these seasick people. I can't go back to my own tiny stateroom on the other side of the boat. The two women I'm sharing it with have been groaning and heaving in their double berth since I got on board in the middle of the night.

My last trip up to the Soo couldn't have been more different. It was a few summers ago—Mother had sent us off to spend the summer with her sister. Jonathan and I were so excited. We'd never taken such a long trip alone. I'd convinced myself that it was the beginning of the rest of my life. Another overly dramatic view of things, I know. But the trip was deathly dull, the water still as glass for the entire voyage. It's hard to believe now, as we're being tossed around like a wooden raft, that I actually wished for some waves just to break up the monotony.

The first mate was kind to us on that journey. We were children traveling alone, but I still think he went beyond the call of duty. He gave us a tour of the pilothouse and showed us where the wheelsman stands to cushion the blow of the captain's shouts. He took us down into the engine room, where men with faces blackened by coal feed the hungry boiler. But what I remember most vividly was how in the middle of Georgian Bay, on the big open water, you couldn't see land in any direction, just water everywhere. It felt as if we were on the ocean. I'm not sure why Georgian Bay is called a bay at all, since it's vast, nearly as big as some of the other Great Lakes. Standing in the small wooden pilothouse looking over the endless water made me dizzy. I wondered how the ship's captain could possibly know where he was without land or rocks or a lighthouse to mark his passage. There's talk every day in the papers about building new lighthouses, putting in buoys and markers for this route, but until then, the mate told us, the steamer captains steer by ear, by nose and by God.

Land finally appeared on the other side of the bay in the morning. It looked to me like a landscape drawn by a child. All craggy rock islands, tiny wizened cedars. The ports we stopped in on the eastern edge—Parry Sound, French River, Killarney—places sailors like my cousin Peter talk about as if they're the bustling centers of the known world, are actually hardscrabble little villages. Shanties instead of houses. Barely a properly dressed person to be seen, though I saw lots of men who looked desperate, untamed, with shaggy beards and no hats. Lumbermen, trappers, fishermen. Sault Ste. Marie isn't much to speak of either. More churches than people, as far as I could tell. Not even a real town, not officially. My aunt told us that in winter the snowdrifts sometimes climb over the doorframes, and people get lost trying to reach the loo behind their home. Others are locked inside for weeks on end, eating canned meat and old potatoes. She didn't stay up there for long.

I hope I can bear it. I've never liked the cold, but the Soo is the only place I can think of to disappear to. Surely anything is better than rotting away at home without Jonathan, the stench of despair thick as fog in our house.

I sometimes think if I ran into myself now—if I met the girl I was on that summer voyage, or even a few months ago, before everything happened—I'd want to slap her across her silly little mug, tell her to get a grip on herself, tell her that life isn't what happens in books. Life isn't a bowl of ice cream, as Mother never fails to remind me. I used to think it was cruel of her to say this, as if she wanted to ruin things for me so I'd be more like her: tired and disappointed and old. But now I know it to be true.

I move forward toward an open area and down another set of stairs. The boat lists to port, and a huge traveling trunk painted blue with a metal frame breaks free of its tether and slides in front, nearly knocking me off my feet. The trunk bashes against the side of the boat, then, as the ship stabilizes, slides back to center and stops. I lean down to shove it back toward the wall, grab and retie the rope that was holding it, then sit on top. May as well. It might be the only place where I can get away from everyone.

I can smell something cooking, but it's the last thing I want. I'm starting to feel sick myself now. I've always been the one with the iron-clad stomach. It was Jonathan who got seasick. Even on that calm summer trip up to the Soo, he was doubled over every time the boat heeled gently to one side. It sounds unkind, but it struck me as kind of funny, considering how much he loved to sail and fish. I teased that he had the belly of a landlubber whenever I had a chance.

I shake my head. I don't want to think about Jonathan. I don't want to think about how mean I could be. How he tolerated me—loved me—despite what I said, what I did. How he would look, in fact, as if he pitied me when I said something especially unkind. I don't want to think about it now. I rub my face and lean against the wall of the boat.

We're not rolling so much anymore, and I settle in. Feeling the buzzing of the steam engine against my temple, I have that heavy, comforting feeling I get on a train, as if my body is moving in time with the rhythm of the engine. I close my eyes and drift away on a dream.

Two

The steamer heels heavily to port, and my head slams against the wall. I see stars. A group of women and children huddle on the deck nearby. They look like a flock of birds, four clucking mothers and their hungry, crying babies. I blink a few times, rub my face with my hands. The women are all young but have the haggard, lined faces of people who've spent their lives outside. Two of them look especially ill, their skin almost yellow.

I don't have to move. They're gypsies, travelers. No one would ask me to give up my seat on the trunk. Still, I think of Jonathan. He was always looking out for the unfortunate. I straighten my hat and hair, pat down my stiff black mourning dress and get up. I can't sit here any longer anyway. And I don't want to be around squalling children. The women look at me dolefully and nod but don't say anything. One of them stumbles when she tries to stand up. She gives up altogether and crawls on her hands and knees over to the trunk;

then, instead of getting up on top of it, collapses with her back against the metal.

I keep walking. Movement is reassuring. I need to move.

The trunk makes me think of that man waiting in line behind me last night while the ship was tied up in Owen Sound harbor. He was angry long before he boarded the ship. I tried to avoid eye contact. I didn't want to hear his complaints, and besides, if I'm going to disappear, I can't have anyone remembering me. Still, it was impossible not to listen. I could feel the hot charge of his fury even in the dark. Once we got to the deck, he dropped his heavy metal trunk and stormed around yelling. He didn't care whom he woke up, didn't care that everyone around him just wanted to tuck into bed. It was midnight, and he insisted on a refund for his ticket because of how full the ship was. He slammed his foot down, waved his arms about, telling the poor crewman— a boy younger than me—that he wouldn't trust his pet budgie to such a boat. He made accusations about Captain Savage, the shipping company, the government, for goodness' sake. He left the ship in a huff, dragging his trunk behind him. I wrote him off as a lunatic at the time, but here in the middle of a storm, with everyone on board throwing up, cargo flying around and the boat lurching from one side to the other, I wonder if he might have been the sanest person on the docks.

I make my way toward the front of the boat again, hand over hand on the railing, trying to keep my balance. Two men are arguing in the open passageway at the top of the stairs. I can't hear their words, but they sound angry, unhinged, as if there is nothing to lose. I stop to catch my breath. I'd like to loosen my corset. I put it on in a hurry this morning, and it's far too tight for comfort. But that would require going back to my room. I tuck strands of wet hair under my hat and inhale deeply.

"I can't do it!" I hear one of them say. "I won't. Not anymore."

"You don't have a choice," the other says, his voice carried to me on the wind. "You're mine. I *own* you."

I edge closer. There's nothing accidental about it— I'm definitely eavesdropping now. At least it's a distraction from the pitching and rolling, from the puke and dread of the other passengers. I lean into the wall of cabins, flattening myself to the wood, straining to hear.

"You do *not* own me. You don't get to decide what I do. I'm not a child anymore."

I can't see the two men, but the last one *sounds* like a child—or, at least, not yet a fully grown man. There is a quaky pitch to his voice. Still, he is certain of what he's saying, like he's been practicing these words for a while.

"Who do you think bought those clothes you're wearing? Who puts the food in your mouth, you ungrateful *boy*?" The man spits out this last word like a curse.

"I am *not* a boy. And I'm telling you I won't do it anymore."

"You think you're not a part of this? You think your hands are clean?"

Now things are getting interesting. I find myself rooting for the boy with the quaky voice, his defiance of the older man's demands. I edge over to see if I can get a better view, but they're tucked inside, away from the cold spray that's turning me into a frozen statue. I can't see them without them seeing me.

"I don't care," the younger one says loudly. "I can't do it anymore. I won't. I'll...I'll tell the police. I don't care what you say."

"Is that right?" the older one says, with an unpleasant laugh. "You think that's a good idea, do you?"

But then there's a dull thud, the smack of skin against skin, and some foot shuffling. "Hey!" the older man says.

I can't help myself. I step away from the wall to see what's happening, and as I do, someone runs right into me.

I stumble and catch myself on the guardrail, grabbing my hat before I lose it. I gasp, feeling a stab of something between expectation and indignation. But the boy—and it *is* a boy, about the same age as me—doesn't speak, doesn't apologize. His face is a crudely drawn mask. I can't read it at all. He offers me his hand, and I grasp it, trying to regain my dignity. He pulls me up, and we're standing nearly face-to-face. Not a word passes between us. He's tall and reedy, a thin nose, angular features. Some would say handsome. He raises one eyebrow, and the hint of a smile flickers in his eyes. My mouth is dry. I don't have any words. He drops my hand and bows at the neck, tipping his hat at me.

But this gesture doesn't feel like an apology at all. It feels, in fact, like arrogance. I'm about to say something, something to let this boy know I'm not a person who can be knocked down without a proper account, not a woman to be toyed with. But before I can speak, he tilts his bony shoulder against the wind and water and walks purposefully toward the stern.

I pull myself up more fully and reach for the safety of the wooden wall again, watching him retreat. His boots thump loudly on the deck.

I'm still trying to collect myself, trying to figure out if I'm more insulted or curious, when the other man steps out of the doorway. He holds onto the frame of the entranceway with both hands. "You won't get away with this!" he calls out, practically yelling in my face.

Maybe I *have* become invisible. I take a step toward him, so he can't help but notice me, can't help but know I've witnessed this exchange. The man is also tall and thin, but while the boy had a gentle look, something soft in his mouth, his eyes, this man is too thin, flimsy somehow. He might have once been handsome, but now he's all sharp edges. He touches the brim of his hat and looks at his feet. "My apologies, Miss…"

The man doesn't wait for me to respond, just turns on his heel and slips back through the doorway.

I'm puzzling through all this, smarting from nearly being knocked to the deck, from the boy's presumption, when the boat leans so far to starboard I think it might roll over entirely this time. I brace myself, but we bounce back, and I scramble to regain my footing, catch my breath. There's a stillness in the steamer that feels like anticipation.

I grip the doorframe. The boat seems to settle.

I'm not sure if I've just witnessed a family spat or the end of a criminal partnership. Is it something grave and big and terrible or something meaningless, the sort of argument that happens in families—my family—all the time, quickly forgotten, never revisited.

I consider following the boy—anything to keep my mind off the sick people everywhere and their wailing and crying—but I'm stopped by a thunderous clatter of hooves. There's a deep, guttural moan coming from the cows on the front deck, like a choir of the damned. We heel over deeply once again.

A heaviness fills my belly, and my arms hang from my shoulders like iron weights. All I can hear is the rush of blood in my head. We bob upright again. I stand as still as I can on the deck, looking toward the noise, listening for the sound of hooves, more moans, not wanting to believe what my heart is telling me. Not wanting to believe that the cows above us are being pushed overboard, that the crew is panicking about the storm.

The steamer is surprisingly quiet again, as if the engines have been shut off, as if all of us onboard are holding our collective breath, hoping that what we think happened didn't. Then I hear animals again. The boat heels one more time, leaning over like a footman's bow, this time the movement accompanied by the high-pitched shrieks of horses as they unmistakably plunge into the frigid water.

I start running, though I don't know where to go. People are everywhere. Dishes are crashing against the walls of cabins as the boat rolls back. A woman screams. A child shouts: "Mama!" I see a man in a dark suit and white minister's collar talking to a group of people gathered near another set of stairs. They are holding hands, praying. The minister has a heavy palm on the shoulder of a man who is like a hot-air balloon about to launch into the sky. The preacher keeps him grounded, counsels patience, calm. I push past them, lifting up my heavy dress hem to take the stairs two at a time. Someone tries to grab my arm, but I don't stop. I need to get up higher. I need to see the horizon, see the water, find something to hold on to with my eyes.

At the top of the stairs on the hurricane deck, people are pulling on life preservers that have been packed tightly in boxes near the lifeboats. I take one from the pile, tug it on, fumbling with the laces. It's already wet and heavy. The neck pulls at my hair and the shoulders of my dress.

Water lashes the deck. It's not safe here. There's no proper shelter other than inside the wheelhouse. The boat is rolling madly now, and I grip the guardrail to head back down the stairs. Something—an instinct? a premonition?—tells me I must get to my stateroom. I don't even knock, just push inside. The door won't open all the way, and I have to squeeze past debris scattered over the floor. The women are gone. I sink down onto the single bed and look around the small space. Clothes and luggage are everywhere. The porcelain water jug and large saucer with the faint daisy pattern are in pieces on the floor. I consider picking up the shards, an urge my mother would be pleased to witness, but then realize tidying up right now would be absurd. Pure madness.

"Chris? Christina?" My cousin Peter bursts into the room, gripping each side of the doorframe, water pouring in over the threshold at the bottom. "You found a life preserver," he says. "Good."

"Is it going to last?" I ask.

"Let's hope not," he says, his face oddly expressionless. "But prepare yourself for the worst. The lifeboats are on the hurricane deck. Listen for the horn."

He slams the door behind him.

Time slows inside my small cabin. I feel sealed off from the storm outside, from the panic and puke of my fellow passengers. *Lifeboats. Hurricane deck.* My cabinmates must have left in a hurry, because one of the women has abandoned her leather-bound journal on the bed. I'd read it if the boat weren't rocking so much I can hardly see. I glance around the room, but my eyes aren't able to settle on anything, and I find my mind drifting, searching for comfort, for a story that makes sense.

It's something I do often since Jonathan died. I'm here but not here. I land on a sleigh ride the whole family took at my grandmother's house last Christmas, snowfall lighting up the moonlit sky. There was an argument, of course, before the horses were hitched. Should Jonathan come with us? Should he stay? And who would stay with him? I waved them all away and insisted he come. I told them they were altogether too meddlesome. And Jonathan was pleased with my insistence, I know he was, though he'd never make such a fuss himself.

Sitting on my berth in a rocking boat, in the middle of what feels increasingly like a hurricane, I disappear into the sparkling winter sky of that Christmas night, my twin brother beside me, cozy beneath the heavy fur and woolen blankets. And I think this must be what dying feels like—comfort and fear at the same time, an inescapable slide into nothingness.

But then the boat heels deeply to starboard, and I leap to my feet. I have to do something. I have to get out.

All I have considered lately is death and dying—my brother's, my own—and yet here I am, faced with the possibility of drowning, of disappearing into the blue, and I have the unmistakable urge to live. It surprises me, but I can't sit here thinking about sleigh rides and snowflakes a second longer.

I bang on the door adjoining the next stateroom and push inward with all my weight. The wood strains and cracks.

There's a woman with her two young children, a babe in arms and another about two years old. Both children are whimpering, but their mother is lying on her berth, corset untied, eyes open. The small space smells like vomit. I push the children aside and shake her, gently at first, then more forcefully, but she barely acknowledges me. I tell her she must get life preservers, save her children. The woman groans but doesn't move, looking at me with heavy-lidded eyes. I need to find Peter, ask him to help. What can I do with two small children and a sick woman?

I squeeze out, and the door slams behind me. I'm short of breath—I can't inflate my lungs with air. My hat is gone. Where is my hat? I stumble, fall over and land hard on another door. This one doesn't give way. The steamer itself, in fact, seems to have heeled even more to starboard, settling there. I hear a crack. Something shifts, creaks. I'm lying on my back, disoriented, before I realize the boat must be on its side. Water is everywhere. People are shouting, shrieking. The wind is a scream of a higher pitch. I hear the horn blast its lament, engines still churning away. The staterooms on the other, lower side of the boat must be filling with water. The boat is going down.

I force myself to focus. I've got to get out of here. I've got to look for the lifeboats. *The hurricane deck. Prepare for the worst.* I repeat Peter's words in my head like a song. *Hurricane deck, lifeboats, prepare for the worst.* I try to stand up, but it feels like I'm being pushed backward. Up is no longer up. Another door along the promenade deck opens, and I see a man pull himself with the strength of his upper body out of the entranceway as if it were a hole in the floor. He has managed to get one leg out when a wave crashes over us both. I take a deep breath and hold on tight. The water is numbingly cold.

I sputter, spit out water. Wet hair covers my face, and I shove it away. The man is gone. The boat exhales another deep, low shudder. I hear a terrible tearing sound and then watch in horror as the wheelhouse and the rest of the upper works shear off from the rest of the boat. We sink lower in the water.

There's another man, hatless, coatless, nearly close enough to touch. He reaches out a hand, shouts to me, then jumps, disappearing into the darkness.

My breath comes out like a coughing, choking engine. Water is everywhere, and it's so cold I feel as if I'm turning into one of the big blocks of ice we keep covered in sawdust in the icehouse. Nothing makes sense. Everything is sideways, upside down. I'm like a fat frozen spider in my life preserver, scuttling frantically through a topsy-turvy world of doorways where floors should be, seeking higher ground. But what am I looking for? There's no reason to stay with the ship. It's going to sink. And I'm going with it.

I stumble, hitting my head on the guardrail. I can't tell up from down. People are jumping, shouting orders, directions. Others are immobilized with terror, aimless, as if hoping for someone or something to pluck them from this nightmare. I'm dazed too, but something inside me, that same propulsive engine, keeps me moving. I take a step, but my boots slip from underneath me, and I begin to slide. My mouth is open, and a scream emerges that doesn't feel like my own. It is a deep, guttural utterance. An instinct. A plea. I slide past a screaming woman. I'm picking up speed, banging against

doors and windows. I squeeze my eyes shut. I don't want to
see where I'm going to land. What I will hit. I clench my teeth,
draw my shoulders to my ears, brace myself.

But the landing is soft. Icy cold. I try to kick the water,
claw with my hands. I kick again and again, just like Jonathan
and I learned to do hanging onto the dock in Owen Sound
when we were children. I'm frantic, going nowhere. I'm being
pulled under. Water presses into my nose, into my screaming
mouth. I try to fight it, but I can't. *Why me?* My lungs are so
tight they will burst. I can't see anything. It's like looking at
the back of my own eyelids. I hear only the shudder of my
heart. *Why me?* The words are the only thing in my brain.

But something makes me kick again and cup my hands to
draw water. Kick. Kick. I feel no resistance but rise up anyway.
Air. I gasp and sputter. Air. But then I'm hit with a wave and
take in another mouthful of water. I try to tilt my head back.
My boots and dress are heavy stones dragging me downward.
I hear a shout. My name. I open my eyes and see only my
own hair. A wave hits me, and I sink again. The silence is all-
consuming. I can't breathe. I have nothing left. My head, my
lungs, are going to explode.

But there is something else.

Why me?

I fight again, kick with both legs. Claw with both hands.
Kick. Claw. Something touches my shoulder. A knife in my
lungs. I grab something. I see white flesh tinged blue. I reach
toward it and am pulled like the lightest of weights into the
air. It feels like flying.

Three

Jonathan looks gaunt lying in a large pine box in the front room, the curtains drawn, the room stifling. His face is so thin, he's like a skeleton I once saw at the fall fair, bones looped together with copper wire, eyes dark pits. He's trying to whisper something to me, but only a raspy sound emerges. There's a deep cut in the middle of his bottom lip, and the edges are white and raw, the wound oozing blood. But I'm not disgusted. I want to kiss his cold forehead, hold his precious hand. I lean in closer, and he grasps my wrist tightly. He squeezes so hard, I shout.

My eyes are flooded with light. Someone is shaking me. His hand around my wrist. I'm not in the front room at all.

"Wake up, Christina. Wake up. You mustn't sleep," Peter says, his face close to mine. My head is on his shoulder. My entire body tenses, and I shake involuntarily from head to toe. I drift off again. I try to fight it, but I'm so tired. Cold. So cold. I've never felt this kind of exhaustion. Peter shakes my shoulder again. I glance around. There must be twenty people squeezed together in the lifeboat. We're packed like oysters in a tin. Desperate faces. Pale skin, sunken eyes, blood everywhere. People are whimpering, crying, moaning in pain, calling out for their lost children, lost wives, calling out for help. Others look dazed, hair stuck to their faces, shivering in the cold.

It's hard to tell the water from the sky. The *Asia* is nowhere to be seen, although there is a lot of debris in the churning water around us: splintered wood and boxes, barrels and furniture. Waves roll and smash our boat, the storm playing with our small vessel like a cat bats at a mouse. At least we have oars, which is more than I can say for the other two lifeboats I see bobbing helplessly in the huge waves.

Someone near me throws up with a loud retching sound, as if they are being turned inside out. The smell makes my own stomach clench and my throat fill. I close my eyes. Someone else shouts that a wave is gathering. The men with the oars start to row frantically as the tower of water barrels toward us, unstoppable, until it's hovering over the boat, and all of us are cowering, bracing for its weight. But it collapses in on itself just before we're swamped. The spray is hard and bitter as we drift over the high fallen crest. Some of the men try to stabilize the boat. "LEAN STARBOARD!" they call, more joining in like a chant. "Lean starboard!" "Lean starboard!" They seem to be on fire, these men, energized by the crisis.

They row hard—but to where, I have no idea. There is nothing around us, just the raging lake on all sides. I see more debris now, timbers and wooden boxes, bedsheets and hats, pieces of wood from the boat that are barely recognizable.

One of the cabin boys sitting near me points to the spot on the tortured surface of the bay that's swirling hard like water down a drain. "The *Asia*," he says to no one in particular. Captain Savage, who has said little and seems as confused and terrified as the rest of us, comes to life when he hears this, commanding the men to keep rowing away from the ship, lest it pull us under with it.

I don't know how any of them can do anything. My lungs are on fire, and my brain is spinning. It feels like I'm still drowning, like I can't get enough air into my body. I inspect my arms and face for injury, but there's nothing I can see or feel. My hands are wrinkly and strange, like they belong to another, much older me. I can barely feel any sensation in them.

There are people in the water too. Some are floating facedown in life preservers. Others cling to pieces of the wreck, lips blue, eyes wide and hollow with fear. One or two call to us, but our lifeboat is already more than full. There are those in the boat who beg Captain Savage and my cousin to save them, but most of us are quiet, our own survival far from certain.

"We were close to Manitoulin Island when we foundered," Peter says quietly to me, his voice even, emotionless, as if he's speaking only to reassure himself that he is alive. "Unless we were farther off course than I knew…"

I wait for him to say something more, but he just stares at the gathering waves. The water sloshes around the bottom of the lifeboat. It's nearly up to my knees, lapping onto my legs beneath my dress. I start shivering again and can't stop. Peter leans his shoulder into me, as if the pressure from his body will stop the cold. I try to still my stuttering jaw, but it belongs to someone else. Even when I hold my mouth closed with one hand, my teeth chatter together.

I can see the two women I shared the stateroom with sitting toward the back of the boat. They are bareheaded, without their shawls, as I am, exposed to the wind. They nod dully when they see me. The spray from a wave drenches us again, and I can see one of the women moan, but there is nothing to say to comfort her.

The mother and children I saw in the stateroom next to mine aren't in this boat. I can't imagine they escaped. Not the way she looked. My cheeks flood with heat. I should have grabbed the children while I still could.

The men never stop rowing. Some people cheer them on, call out for them to "stroke, stroke, stroke!" But then we see one of the other lifeboats flip over in a wave. We cry out, helpless to do anything. The boat and its cargo disappear into the tossing water. I bury my face in my life preserver. I can't watch. When I look up, the boat has righted itself, but there is no one inside.

An older woman beside me with red cheeks stops moaning and begins crying outright. I lean away from her, as if her despair might be contagious.

We watch helplessly as people try to climb into the righted boat. It's twenty, maybe twenty-five feet long, about the same length as ours, and even before anyone gets in, it's obvious the boat is sitting low in the water. One man hauls himself in at the stern, then tries to help others. The gunwales are nearly submerged. Some cling desperately to the sides. Others try to grab on to each other. There are flailing hands, splashing water. One man still in the water has two people gripping his shoulders, eyes wild, tearing at his life preserver. He is sinking from their weight, and they try to clamber on top of him. They nearly drown him, but he manages to push them off and get up onto the boat. He stands up, his narrow chest heaving in and out, then pulls off his life preserver, throws it to the people in the water and quickly dives off the side. He swims toward us.

His strokes are strong, his eyes never leaving our boat. No one says a word, but it's clear that this one man might be more than our lifeboat can take. And what if others see him and try to do the same? This man's need to survive could easily mean all of our deaths. The captain leans toward Peter and speaks in hushed tones, then sits back up and commands the men on the oars, "Help him."

The crewman closest to the swimmer reaches out an oar, and the man pulls himself along the length of the long blade. His hair is dark, his face dripping, lips moving like a fish out of water. When he is pulled into our lifeboat, I realize he's not a man at all but the boy I saw arguing on the ship. The one who knocked me down. He's still wearing his boots and has a dark jacket that clings to his thin frame. He lies on the bottom of the lifeboat for a long time, eyes wide, chest rising and falling. I watch him struggling to recover, though he doesn't look as if he's been wounded, unlike many of the bloodied survivors in our boat. One of the cabin boys talks to him, but there's nothing to be done. Already we know he will live or die and no one can do anything about it. The men continue rowing.

I watch the boy as he struggles to gain his breath, taking in the contours of his cheeks, the hollow beneath the bone, his pale skin and aristocratic nose. His face is smooth, flawless even, not yet the suggestion of a mustache on his upper lip. His clothes stick closely to his frame. He doesn't look like the kind of person who goes around pushing other people. He doesn't look like someone who could stand up for himself at all. I can't even imagine what he and the other man were fighting about, though the anger was real, their words fueled by a powerful fury.

I've given up wondering when I see the boy lick his lips and swallow, then croak, "My uncle? Have you seen my uncle? Did he make it?"

His uncle. That makes sense. The two looked a bit alike. But is the boy asking because he's hoping to see the other man or because he doesn't want to? I can't tell from his voice. Peter, who's closest to him, shakes his head and looks away.

"It's no use anyway," Peter says to no one in particular.

The rest of us watch as the other lifeboat tips over again. This time when it rights itself, there is no one left to get inside.

When the boy has recovered enough to sit upright, Peter instructs him to move toward the stern to keep the boat balanced. He must climb over other men and women, careful not to tip the boat in the process. "Excuse me," the boy says shakily, "excuse me," as if he were a waiter at a fancy dress party, as if unaware that all decorum went down with the ship. I can't decide if he's putting on a show, delirious or possibly unclear about where we are, what's happened. Maybe he's in shock. He settles into a bench at the back of the boat and looks around with an open face, eyes glassy. All the purpose and ferocity I saw after he pushed the other man on the *Asia*, all the arrogance of his smile and tip of the hat, seem to have disappeared into the churning lake.

Our boat is stable, considering the number of people and the amount of water in it, considering the fact that the waves are not decreasing, that the wind is a banshee shrieking in our ears. I'm looking around, trying to make sense of where we are and what's going on, when, without warning, a wave the height of a two-story house crests over us. A curtain of water descends. We're thrown to the side, and the boat heels wildly. It seems to pause momentarily, uncertain whether to flip over or return to stability.

The lifeboat flips over. This time the landing isn't soft at all. I smash hard into the water, as if hitting a brick wall. There are bodies, arms, legs, wood, water everywhere. I flail, trying to get away, fighting an unseen, unseeable enemy. I can't be sure which way is up, but I kick and claw anyway. I'm propelled again by this surprising urge to breathe, to survive, despite months of praying that it would be me who died instead of my twin brother.

My head is out of the water. I can see other people, waves pummeling all of us. I take in a mouthful, spit it out, cough, choke. I can see our righted boat, empty, not ten feet away. Some men are already clinging to the sides, negotiating how they will get in without tipping again. Others hang on to bits of wreckage, spars from the *Asia*, fragments of wood.

My heavy dress drags me downward as if I have a blacksmith's anvil tied to my waist. I'm sinking. I try to shout but swallow water. Choke, spit. I don't think I can fight it this time. I am too tired. Too cold. But then the boy from the boat is beside me. He has my left arm in his hand. "Here," he manages to say. "Keep your head up. I'll help you."

And without knowing how it happened, I'm back in the boat, colder even than before. There are fewer people now. Peter made it, but the women from my stateroom are gone. One of the cabin boys is holding up the captain, who can barely keep his eyes open. The cabin boy himself has a gash on his forehead that is leaking blood like a tap. We have only one long, heavy, essentially useless oar.

"Move to the bow," Peter whispers to me, his voice grave. "Hold on to the lifeline rope. If the boat goes over again, hold on tighter than you've ever held on to anything in your life. Don't let go. The lifeboat will right itself, and you'll stay with it."

I barely have the energy to stand up, but Peter pulls me to my feet. I drag myself and my sopping-wet, hundred-pound dress to the bow. The people in the lifeboat don't even move when I pass them. They barely look up. There's so much blood, it's hard to tell where their wounds are. The lifeboat is a battle-field. No one says a word.

When I reach the bow, I grab the rope Peter told me to hold, then sink to the wooden floor of the boat and squeeze myself in. It is a tiny wedge of space. The wind slowly begins to die out, though the waves remain high. We roll up and then down, up and down, and I start to feel seasick again. I can't feel my feet.

I peer over the gunwales, searching for the horizon to still my stomach. That's what everyone used to tell Jonathan to do when he felt seasick. Lock your eyes on the horizon. *Jonathan.*

There have been other moments these past few months when I have forgotten him for a minute, a second. At first I thought that to forget him even briefly was shameful, a black mark on my already questionable character. But what does guilt matter now? What do regrets count for? And who is counting? My nausea rolls in and out.

I'm closing my eyes when Peter shouts, "Waaaaave!" Water thrashes us, and the rope I'm holding digs into the flesh of my hands. I can't see or hear anything but the roar of the water pounding our metal boat. When I open my eyes, two of the men sitting near me are gone, swept overboard. A third is standing up, looking into the water as if it might answer a question he has. "Sit down!" someone near me shouts, and the man turns toward the voice. His face is paper white, his eyes unfocused. He mutters something and looks toward the water.

"Noooo!" I scream, but it's too late. He jumps in. All of us watch as the man disappears, then bobs up about a hundred yards from our boat. He's paddling with both hands, frantically trying to keep his head above water. He looks as if he now regrets his decision, but the wind is blowing us away from him.

There's no time to do anything for him or ourselves before the boat flips over again. I keep grasping the rope, and the sharp fibers tear at my skin. I am bashed in and out of the water, then up, like a floating toy in the bathtub. I cough, try to take air into my lungs. My hands ache, and my forearms feel like string pulled tight to fraying, but I'm still with the boat, still alive. My hands grasp the rope like the pincer claws of one of those crayfish we used to try to catch with our bare hands in the summer. I couldn't let go even if I wanted to. It's one of the cabin boys who helps me back into the boat this time. When I finally release my grip, my hands are bleeding.

I count the people left. Captain Savage and the cabin boy, Peter, the mysterious boy at the stern, plus two men wearing sodden woolen suits. Seven. The oars are gone entirely. We drift without speaking, up and down over the rollers. All urgency is gone. That last wave wiped out any sense that we are in control of anything. Nobody speaks. What is there to say? The wind begins to fade as darkness falls like a boulder.

Four

The boy in the stern is talking to me, but his words are gibberish, bird caws, nonsensical noise. He gestures with his hands, leaning forward, as if the sheer force of his motions will make me understand. I stare at him blankly, then look away. I can't make out a single word.

The wind has died out. There are ripples on the water, like a ghostly hand is gently brushing against it—no more whitecaps or waves. Even the rollers that made me feel sick have disappeared.

The two men in suits lean against one another. They look like corpses—pale, mouths agape, eyes unfocused, jackets still buttoned up tight. I watch as the blond one, middle-aged and clean-shaven, turns to the larger man, touching him on the opposite shoulder with a tenderness that surprises me.

The man's lips are moving beneath a dark mustache. "My boy," he says over and over. "My little boy." His head drops to his thick chest, and his shoulders shake. The blond man gently pats him again, then sighs and returns to staring dully into the distance.

The captain, who is positioned closer to me than to the men in suits, seems more confused than ever, startling suddenly when there is no sound, his hands shaking as if he were having a seizure. And Peter, who has been so competent, taking charge of our collective will to live, pushing us along with reports and speculation—the distance to Parry Sound, the height of the closest lighthouse, the number of lifeboats and their capacity—as if information itself will keep us afloat, is also beginning to look like he doesn't know where he is. He is the only person other than the captain who hasn't openly despaired about our fate.

Fate. What ridiculous nonsense I was spouting earlier. I'm embarrassed by my very thoughts. Thinking about facing one's fate head on is perfectly fine when it's theoretical, distant, a glimmer of an idea, not even the idea itself. But now that our fate seems decided, death like a shroud ready to descend, I have lost such certitude. I feel like a child. I want to huddle beneath my mother's skirts or cry into her neck. I want to clutch Jonathan's familiar hand and feel his breath match mine in cadence and depth and intensity. How could I have thought it was a good idea to run away from home?

I shake my head to escape this chatter.

The boy at the other end of the boat raises his hand to me, calls out, his words finally taking proper shape. "My name is Daniel," he says.

A proper introduction seems strange with delirious men drifting in and out of consciousness between us, and yet, as he speaks, it strikes me as equally odd that it's taken so long for us to tell each other our names. It's as if we are not quite human out here.

"Christina," I offer, my voice rough, untested after all these hours.

Daniel nods, looking as if he's about to say more, but Peter groans, and I turn toward my cousin.

"Mary," he says when I lean in close. "Is it you, Mary?"

"No," I whisper, my voice catching in my throat. "It's Christina, your cousin. Mary is your wife. She's safe at home."

"Tell Mary I love her," he says. "Kiss the babies for me."

I try to choke back my fear. "You can bloody well kiss them yourself when we get rescued," I tell him. Mother would say that such language isn't fit even for a lifeboat in a storm, but what does she know?

Before Jonathan became ill, I had never considered that Mother's powers could be limited. She was infallible. She knew the right thing to say in every circumstance, the proper way to do everything, from setting the table to making household budgets to raising money for the poor. I thought sometimes she could read my mind. But in the months before Jonathan died she disappeared. She was there, yes, doting on Jon, carrying water, fetching blankets, but it was as if she were a scarecrow, straw stuffing for a heart, a spine. She shuffled around vacantly, did what was required of her and nothing more. My mother was gone. And yet here she is in my head, admonishing me for cursing.

"Someone will come for us," I say to Peter, though I barely believe it myself anymore. There have to be some alarms being raised. We've surely been drifting for hours. The *Asia* was scheduled to make land by now. There will be talk in Parry Sound and Byng Inlet and points north. Telegrams being sent up and down and back and forth across the bay. Search parties will be launched. Articles written. Handkerchiefs wrung. The company will act quickly, I tell Peter. I don't have to explain why. We both know about the lawsuits, threats, insurance claims. The only reason a riverboat like the *Asia* was doing this trip at all is because the *Manitoulin*, whose route it is, caught fire and ran aground, burned to the waterline, a few short months ago. Eleven souls were lost. I've heard that the captain, the legendary Black Pete Campbell, escaped the burning vessel—the last man off the boat—with a child tucked under his arm.

Peter, the unlucky soul, had been crew on that steamer too. Afterward, his mother—my aunt—and his wife, Mary, begged him not to sail again, to find work on land, to tether himself to another star. But he was not to be persuaded. He said he'd been a sailor all his life and he'd die a sailor, though I'm certain he didn't think it would be so soon. He said the company had powerful incentive to make sure nothing like that ever happened again. He said there were new safety measures. Rules. Regulations. But now...now there will surely be a cry for company heads heard around the country.

Of course, if we don't find land and shelter soon, such a cry won't matter one whit. Rescue after first light probably won't be soon enough for Peter—or for the cabin boy, the captain, the other men or me. We'll all die of exposure or drowning or injuries no one else can see.

I straighten up and pull away from my cousin, rolling my head back and forth to stretch my neck. It creaks like the old back stairs. The man with the mustache catches my eye. He clears his throat, tries to rally.

"Someone will come for us?" he asks, his voice small and pleading for such a big man.

"I think so," I say as kindly as possible. "I hope so."

"My boy. I haven't seen him. Not since...not since the ship...he's small for his age...ten. He's only ten...maybe he's in another lifeboat."

He looks to me for reassurance, and I shrug halfheartedly, then nod again. Still, it seems to encourage him.

"They'll be sending search parties. For me. My boy. My company"—he pauses and takes a deep breath, the very act of inhaling an effort—"will be looking.

"Lumber," he says. "I'm in lumber. The name is Sullivan. Fred Sullivan. We're going to the Island. My boy and me. They're...they're expecting us."

It strikes me with the suddenness of a blow that not a soul other than Peter knows I was even on the *Asia*. No one is expecting me at all. If I die, I will have disappeared into thin air. It's what I thought I wanted, but now the idea of vanishing so entirely makes me feel as lonely as I have ever felt, even in the darkest days after Jonathan's death.

"My boy..." the man says again, as if for the first time. "Have you seen him?" He looks for a second like he's going to cry. His lips quiver, his eyes unfocused.

I saw many children on the ship, but few in the lifeboats. I can't bear to say it. I just shrug and look down at my hands. They aren't bleeding anymore, though the skin is raw.

I'm numb, shocked into dullness. I touch my palms against the metal edge of the boat to feel the sting of cold against my broken skin and remind myself that I am alive.

I lean back down to try to comfort Peter. I beg my cousin to sing a song, hoping it will keep him awake, hoping it will drown out the despair that sounds in my mind like the long, mournful whistle of a train. He always loved to sing at Christmas when we gathered around our grandmother's piano. He has a booming baritone full of richness and depth, like dark molasses. A voice like nothing you'd expect from such a slight man. He would bellow "Good King Wenceslas," tucking his chin into his chest and pumping his arm with the rhythm. I whisper to him about the many Christmases we've spent together, about the one he will have with his young family soon. The twinkling candles and smell of pine. The oranges. Oh, the oranges.

"Here," I say, "smell the orange on my fingertips. The sharp, tart flavor is filling your nostrils, the first juice shocking your tongue." Peter gamely sniffs at my fingers, but his eyes are empty, his breath labored. He mumbles something I can't make out.

Without my noticing, Daniel has moved beside me. He's touching my arm. I look down at his hand, a thick gold watch around his wrist, his fingers on my skin. It feels as if I've woken from some kind of trance, like the sort those faith healers had when Mother hired them as Jonathan was near the end. They looked like any other women you might meet on the street—cheap hats, old-fashioned bustles, shirt-waists. More ordinary than most, possibly, but when the pair of them were at our house, sitting at Jonathan's bedside, his bony hands held in theirs, the women seemed to grow larger. They shouted and sang, fell into a trance, spoke in tongues, swaying with the beat of their passion. One of them anointed my brother's wide, pale forehead with water. They went in and out of what looked like a fevered state, though their eyes were wide-open. Then *snap*, the trance ended as quickly as it had begun, the way blowing out a candle sinks a room suddenly into darkness.

"You must keep him awake," Daniel says to me. "The mate. Talk to him."

"I am," I say. "I haven't stopped talking. All I'm doing is talking. To Mr. Sullivan. To Peter. I'm trying to get him to sing."

Daniel looks at me strangely, as if he doesn't believe me. I can't imagine why he'd doubt my words, why he'd suggest with his raised eyebrows and wrinkled nose that I am lying or mad. But maybe I *am* mad. I feel untethered, adrift.

"All right then. Keep talking. It's starting to get dark, and the others don't look well. I think the cabin boy is dead. Mr. McAllister is looking rough too."

It's my turn to look at him with eyebrows raised.

"Him," Daniel says, pointing to the blond businessman. The man's pocket watch is hanging out of his coat, and his eyes are closed. He could easily be sleeping, though his hands are balled up tight, knuckles white.

"I was talking to him before," he says. "James McAllister. He has a wife, four children. He lives on the island. He's a shoemaker, he told me. He was in Owen Sound buying leather. I tried to get him to keep talking, to keep his eyes open. But he closed them, and now he isn't breathing anymore."

"Are you sure?"

Daniel looks at me with what seems like contempt. "Well…I held my hand in front of his mouth and couldn't feel anything. I watched his chest. It's not rising or falling."

He's speaking very close to my face, and I shift in my seat, leaning away. I'm not sure what to make of him. It seems as if he doesn't recognize me from the boat. Maybe he was so angry when he knocked into me that I didn't even register. Perhaps I imagined his cheeky smile.

Still, I'm not comfortable being so close. I lean farther away and the boat rocks.

"Hey there. Careful!" Daniel shoots me a poisonous look.

"Sorry," I say. He's erratic too. Edgy.

"I should go back to the stern. Keep the boat balanced," he says.

"Right. I'll talk to Pe—the mate," I say, not ready to reveal my connection to Peter with this strange, changeable boy. "And to Captain Savage. I'll talk to him too."

I glance at the captain, who looks like a soggy, deflated Saint Nicholas now, with his white beard and belly. He's sitting on the floor of the boat, legs out, exposing his sagging socks and white ankles. He acknowledges us with a tilt of his chin, eyelids at half-mast. Mr. Sullivan is slumped over as well.

"I wish we had a bailer," Daniel calls when he's settled down in the back.

"Pardon me?"

"To bail water? To empty the boat?" He raises his eyebrows as if I'm thick.

"Right. Yes. A bailer." I feel like a fool. But I'm too tired to protest. Too tired to defend myself. The water in the boat is nearly up to the benches. My feet are numb.

"All right," he says. "And don't fall asleep yourself. Even if you think you can't stay awake. Call to me. Talk to me. Talk to the others. We can keep each other awake. Alive."

I watch carefully as Daniel speaks. What I thought was gentle, possibly even handsome, about his face when I first saw him now seems as sharp as his uncle. With everything around us ground down by cold and water, wind and horror, he seems remarkably undulled. I shiver again. I try to remember exactly what I overheard on the boat. The other man said the boy was part of whatever awful thing they'd done. What if it's theft they were discussing? Or worse... murder? I push the thought away into the murk of my mind. I hug my arms around my chest and resolve to focus on my cousin.

"Come on, Peter. Sing for me. I know you love to sing." I gently shake his arm.

Peter's head rolls back. He groans and lazily opens, then closes his eyelids. I see the whites of his eyes traced with red veins, and I try to shake him again, but he's not to be revived. Panic flickers through my arms and legs.

I lean over the edge of the boat to look into the water. I've never thought of water as anything more than a simple, useful substance, something I drink, swim in, float upon. Now the water itself seems cruel. Cold and fathomless and full of malice. I watch the wind build up small waves that collapse gently, rustlings on the surface. The open water goes on forever.

Behind the boat something glints and disappears. I search for it again, but there's nothing there. I must be imagining it. Now *I'm* hallucinating.

But there it is again. A flicker in the water. Something floating. It might be a corpse, or a fragment of the boat that failed us. What little light remains in the sky has begun to leak away.

It's an oar. "Over here!" I shout toward Daniel.

He follows the direction of my hand and moves quickly toward the middle of the boat. He leans over and fishes the long wooden oar out of the lake. The wood is splintered along its ten-foot length, but the narrow blade is mostly intact. Instead of using it, though, Daniel sighs and wedges it between the gunwales and a bench, blade in the air. I can feel the thump of wood against the metal hull through my boots. He sits down resignedly, breathing hard.

"What are you doing? Can't we use it?"

The oar is the first good news we've had since we got in the boat. Why isn't he taking advantage? "Is it too broken?"

I can see the captain nodding almost imperceptibly at me, though he says nothing aloud.

"I'm tired," Daniel says. "I just need to rest a bit—I could hardly lift it out of the water…and I don't know how we'll use just one. We'll go in circles."

I'm about to speak, about to say that I'll give it a try, when Peter suddenly sits up. There is light in his eyes for the first time in hours, though he's weirdly unfocused, like he's in a dream. He straightens himself and takes a deep breath. I have a feeling something awful is going to happen. He's going to jump overboard like that other man, or curse maybe, perhaps scream at me or Daniel.

But instead my cousin sings. *"Pull for the shore, sailor!
Pull for the shore."* His deep voice is resonant even now.
He has to brace himself against the bench to stay upright,
but the lifeboat rings with the rich flavors of his voice.

*"Heed not the rolling waves, but bend to the oar;
Safe in the lifeboat, sailor, cling to self no more!"*

Even though Peter is more animated than he's been for
hours, and he sings more brightly than I've ever heard the old
hymn sung, it still feels like a dirge, a lament. I can feel every
word in my body like wind shaking the boughs of a tree.

"Leave the poor old stranded wreck, and pull for the shore!"

Peter's voice trails off a bit toward the end, though his eyes
still shine like a fever. When he's finished, Captain Savage
thumps his hand weakly on the metal hull of the boat as if in
agreement. Mr. Sullivan adds his thump to the chorus. Peter's
burst of song has awakened them. But Peter has nothing more
to give. He slouches over, then sinks onto the floor of the boat.
He closes his eyes without saying another word. His breath is
ragged, rattling his chest, the sound a mouse makes scurrying
around the kitchen floor at night.

Daniel has been watching and listening to Peter as carefully as I have. He waves his hand at me to indicate I should
encourage more such activity. And yet he still doesn't take up
the oar. What's wrong with him?

I scowl and turn back to Peter. My cousin's eyes are
squeezed shut, as if determined not to let in any light.

"I'll sing, too, if you don't open your eyes," I threaten, only
half teasing. "You know how bad that will be."

I'll do it if it will revive him again—though even here, in
the middle of a storm in the middle of Georgian Bay, my voice

embarrasses me. It's a family joke. Jonathan told me it is worse than a murder of crows.

He always had a way with words. He said he wanted to be a poet. He loved the Greeks. Homer's epics, doused in myth and story. He wrote long, heroic stories and poems of his own too. Mother and Father discouraged this, of course. He was supposed to go to medical school, though I know he was thinking of teaching or getting a job at a newspaper because he figured it would give him more time to write his poems.

I probably knew Jonathan better than anyone else on the face of the earth, but I never really understood why he loved poetry so much. I like to read well enough, but poetry is too ornamental, too much mooning about flowers and trees and love for my taste. I'm just more practical, I guess. Women are supposed to be the sentimental ones, but in our family, it's reversed. It's Father who loves opera, Jonathan who waxed eloquent about birds on the wing. Mother and I are more concrete.

I've often thought that if life were different, more fair, I suppose, it would be me who they insisted go to medical school. It would be me who studied science. It's not right that girls can't follow what interests them. I took the same classes, studied for the same examinations, but when I got into the Collegiate they insisted I study art, music, French, literature. No math or science, even though there's a fully equipped science lab that's available. If I hadn't dropped out of school last year to be with Jonathan, I might have left anyway. What's the point if I can't do what I want?

I look up at Daniel, who's staring at me as I speak to Peter. I don't know if my efforts to keep him awake are helping at all.

My thoughts bounce in the waves like the lifeboat, up and down, rising and falling. If Daniel takes up the oar, I do not notice. Eyes open, mind far away. Darkness begins to settle over us entirely. It is Mr. Sullivan who startles me out of my daydream this time. He's on his knees on the bottom of the boat, his face lathered in sweat, his dark hair tousled like that of a child who's just woken. He points off the side of the lifeboat. "There! There! Do you see it? A light! We're saved! We're saved!"

I try to follow the line of his hand into the distance, but I can't see anything.

"Do you see it? Do you see the light?" I call to Daniel.

He mouths the word *no*, and I can just make out that he's shaking his head reluctantly. I squint into the glowering darkness, the black of night pressing in on us like an unwanted embrace.

Five

"Are you asleep?" Daniel asks, his voice little more than a whisper.

"Nope," I say, though the truth is, in the deep, dark quiet of this enormous lake it's hard to tell the difference between being awake and asleep.

"Both of the men are dead," he tells me. "The other one isn't breathing now. I don't know what happened."

I don't respond. I try to forget the sound of Fred Sullivan's voice begging me to say I've seen his little boy. What is there to say? We are adrift with corpses, no end in sight. I check the captain and my cousin. Peter's eyes are closed. He looks peaceful, unblemished, like when we were children and played together at our grandmother's house in Owen Sound. He's still breathing. So is the captain, though I haven't seen either of them so much as open their eyes for a long time.

There's a terrible smell coming from somewhere in the lifeboat. A mix of sweat and puke and something new, like a well-used outhouse on a hot day. I try not to breathe through my nose, but it's hard to get enough air. My corset must have loosened in the water, but it's still tight. I untie the life preserver, then sit up and lean away from the smell. I've nearly forgotten about the cold except for my fingers, which are swollen and useless. I long to stand up, to move my body. I think I understand now why that man jumped off the side of the lifeboat. He wanted to escape this ridiculous tin can. He needed to be free.

"The last name is Thompson," Daniel says. "My friends call me Dan."

"McBurney," I say. "My friends call me Chris."

"Pleased to meet you."

I can't help myself. I start to giggle. "Lovely to meet you too," I manage to spit out.

"What's so funny?" he asks.

"I'm sorry. It's absurd, I guess. This situation. You introduced yourself as if we were meeting at a ball, and yet we are in the middle of the bay, with dead bodies at our feet and another hundred drowned below us."

Daniel doesn't say anything. I'm being callous. And I've probably insulted him. There's nothing funny here. And for all I know, he's gone mad. Maybe he was before. Maybe he's been waiting for all of us to die so he can disappear, start a new life. I've heard about people doing that after a shipwreck: vanishing and starting again with a new name, a clean slate.

My mind is a windmill. My icicle fingers crack as I grip the edge of the bench. "I'm sorry," I say. "I'm just frightened. Sometimes I laugh when things aren't funny at all. I can't help myself. It's gotten worse since my brother died."

"That's all right," he says, his voice softening. "This isn't exactly normal. Any of it. I said what I said because I don't know what else to say. I just wanted to be polite." He pauses. "How old was he?"

"Who?"

"Your brother."

"How do you know I have a brother?"

He doesn't speak for a second or two. "You just told me he died?"

"Oh. Sorry. Right." I must be losing my mind. I'm dizzy, confused. "He was the same age as me. Seventeen. We're twins. *Were* twins. He died this spring. That's why I'm running—that's why I'm going to the Soo. My parents couldn't stand looking at me anymore. Jonathan was Mother's favorite. She hates me because I survived."

I'm shocked by the words tumbling out, by this confession about something I haven't even fully admitted to myself. It's as if I can't stop myself, as if I've left all my inhibitions on the sunken ship. I put my hand to my mouth to keep the words in. I can't see Daniel, but I can imagine what he's thinking about me laughing in the middle of this horror, confessing family secrets to a stranger.

But if Daniel's surprised by my words, his voice doesn't give him away. He barely pauses. "My mother had a favorite too," he says. "It was my eldest brother. *Why can't you be more like Joseph?* she would say. After him, I guess we were all a great heaping cup of disappointment. He was the only one she kept around. The rest of us were sent off to live with relatives who supposedly needed our help."

"Oh," I say. I know such things are common, but something about his manner, his fine nose, had made me think he came from a different sort of family. Wealthy maybe. Or at least not the sort of poor folk who have to ship their children off because they can't afford them. "I'm sorry." And yet his confession is also a relief, his words making my own less strange and objectionable.

"So what happened? How did he die?" Daniel asks.

"Consumption," I say, the word catching in my throat like a nettle. I cough. Swallow. "He had it for a long time. He got worse, then better, then worse again. Our mother doted on him. Said his bright eyes and flushed cheeks were *his perfect soul shining through.* But in the end he wasted away. Disappeared, really. I can still hear his cough as if it came from my own throat..." I don't intend to, but I cough again.

"I had a younger sister who had it," Daniel says. "She died too."

The two of us sit in silence. It is so quiet and so dark, we could be anywhere in the world—in the sky, underwater. There is no close or far away, no touching anything, adrift in this boundless space. The boat bounces up and through waves, into troughs and over. The sound of the wind is a long, consistent whistle.

I'm not sure how long we sit there without speaking. I drift from curiosity about this strange boy to wariness and back. He's not what he seems. Each time I think I've got him figured out, he changes. A cold wave splashes the side of the boat, spraying my face, shocking me back to reality. I breathe through my nose deeply as I wipe my cheeks. The terrible smell coming from the dead men hits me again like a punch. "Oh, that's awful," I choke out.

"Uh-hmm," he says. "Awful."

"What about you?" I ask finally. "Where were you going before...before...?"

"Huh?" he says, as if he's been asleep. "Sorry. Where am I going?"

I nod before I realize he can't see me. It doesn't matter.

"You mean...on the *Asia*? My uncle and I were down in Toronto and got on board in Collingwood. We were...we were... buying for the winter. I work with him at his dry goods store in Manitowaning. On Manitoulin Island. Have you been there?"

"No."

"It's mostly rock and swamp," he says. "Lots of farmers. Indians. Good folks. We've got a newspaper though. And a couple of hotels. It's not fancy like Owen Sound, but well... it suits me just fine. We're the only dry goods store in town. We sell food, some clothing, hardware, blankets, candles, oil for lamps—that sort of thing. I'm headed there. I *was* headed there."

"Your uncle? Do you think—is he, is he...?" I can't say it.

Daniel pauses before answering. "Alive? I don't know. I haven't seen him since the boat went down."

"I'm sorry." It seems the proper thing to say, though from what I saw, he is not sorry at all.

"It's all right. I'm not the only one, am I? I'm not the only one who's...lost someone."

I can hear him shuffling himself around on his bench, as if trying to get comfortable. "To tell you the truth, he was a bad man," he blurts out. "My uncle."

I wish I could see Daniel's face. I should tell him that I heard his argument, his shouting, that it was me he ran into. He clearly doesn't remember, and it's dishonest not to say something. And yet I don't even know how to begin. It will sound as if I was deceiving him by not saying something before. And I don't know if I can keep the questions from my voice.

But there's something else too. Something stopping me. It's almost as if everything that happened before this moment, before this aimless drifting in the middle of Georgian Bay, is unreal, disconnected from right now. It is as if we are out of time, out of space. As if we are the only two people left in the world.

I don't speak, and Daniel doesn't either. His words just drift there like low-hanging clouds. *Bad man.*

"I've been trying to figure out," I say finally, forcing myself to speak, "if there are others. Survivors, I mean. There was that one lifeboat you were in before you got in ours. And I definitely saw another one. But they just kept flipping over. I don't know if anyone else made it." I gesture toward the large man who sits now on the floor of the lifeboat with his head resting on the metal side, water lapping at his waist. "Mr. Sullivan has—had a son. A little boy. He said he hoped the child was in another lifeboat. Do you think they could have made it?"

Daniel doesn't answer right away. I can hear him gulp. He sounds close, all of a sudden, like he's right next to me, though he hasn't moved from his spot in the stern.

"Well, I think...I think we might be the only ones. The other lifeboats didn't have flotation under the seats like this one."

The two of us sit in silence, water pushing against the hull, pushing us around, going nowhere.

"What happened?" I ask. I know I don't have to explain what I mean.

"I dunno," he says. "The ship was top-heavy, overloaded, that's for sure. And crowded. Did you see all those animals at the bow? Horses. Cows too, I think. But maybe that kind of storm would knock over any ship. The waves...I've never seen anything like it. I guess only the captain knows for certain," Daniel says. "And he's not doing very well."

I look toward Captain Savage leaning against the bench beside my cousin. My eyes have adjusted to the dark, and I can see his open mouth, jaw loose the way it is with old people when they're asleep. He looks contented, as if he were resting on his own front porch, a warm summer breeze blowing over him.

"He's okay. He's breathing. Can you see anything up there?" I ask. "Land? That light? We've been drifting for hours. Shouldn't we have seen *something* by now? Anything?"

"No," Daniel says. "I don't see nothing—anything..." His voice trails off, and I think he's finished talking until he says, "We'll have to make land at some point."

"Or a shoal. Let's hope we don't hit a shoal," I say, already regretting my doomsaying. Mother always says I can't resist raining on a parade.

"Pardon?"

I shrug. Who am I trying to protect? If there's a time for pessimism, this is it. "I just said let's hope it's not a shoal that we land on. There are lots of rocks just under the surface along the shore. If we're near shore, I mean."

Daniel doesn't respond. "The boat went down around midday," he says. "It gets dark early, so it's probably just before midnight now. That's twelve hours of drifting. I think the wind is blowing from the west or northwest. We'll hit land soon. Maybe Byng Inlet?"

I shiver. "Let's talk about something warm."

"Like what?"

"Well, like how when we're rescued, I'm going to have the hottest bath ever known to man...or woman." I cringe when I realize I've just created a mental image of myself naked in the bath in front of a strange, unpredictable man-boy. "Or maybe how I'm not going to move from in front of the fire," I quickly add. "Tea! We could talk about tea."

"I prefer coffee."

"All right then. Coffee. How do you take it?"

"Milk. Sugar."

"My mother calls tea with milk and sugar Fairy Tea. My brother and I would have the nicest tea parties when we were little, with biscuits and Fairy Tea. What do you think coffee with milk and sugar should be called?"

Daniel pauses.

"You told me to talk if I was having trouble staying awake. I'm talking."

"That's true. But talking about food just makes me more hungry. Why don't you tell me where you're from instead," he says.

My stomach rumbles. "Okay. But I don't think that will help keep me warm." I'm not sure what to tell him. I don't want to confess I'm running away from home. I don't even know what to think about it anymore. The truth is, I didn't stop to consider what it would mean, what I would do when I got to the Soo, what Mother and Father would feel. I just did it. I had to go. I've been running since Jonathan died. Maybe now is as good a time as any to stop.

"I live in Parkdale," I say. "Do you know it? It's west of Toronto, near the water. It's a town, close to the city but not part of it. It's all right. People say it has pretty gardens."

"I was in Parkdale last week," Daniel says. "My uncle goes there all the time. For the store."

"Really?"

"Yeah. It seemed okay. Not much in the way of roads. I was surprised, to tell the truth. I thought it would be... fancier? The houses were nice—grand, some of them— but there was mud and muck and weeds as high as the bottom of the wagon. We went to a glove factory. My uncle has business there. He wanted me to meet some people."

"Uh-huh," I say, not wanting to sound overly curious but hoping he'll continue, that it will help me make sense of what I heard and saw on the ship. But he doesn't say anything more, and I fill in the silence again. "So you work? For your uncle? Do you go to school too?"

"School? No. Not anymore. We don't have anything past the eighth grade on the island. I thought about taking the collegiate entrance exams and going to Owen Sound... but, well...my uncle needed me..."

Without being able to see Daniel's face I'm not sure if I've touched a sore spot or maybe embarrassed him. Most of my friends have done at least a year at the Collegiate or gone to the Normal School to be teachers, but I know it's different in other places. I feel stupid that I've asked, as if I'm some dumb city girl who has no idea how other people live.

"I spent summers here," I offer. "On Georgian Bay. My mother has family in Owen Sound. And the Soo too. I'm going to visit my aunt up there." I clear my throat, the lie burning as I swallow. "Peter, the first mate, is my cousin. Our mothers are sisters."

"Really? I had no idea. He's a good sort. Young for all that responsibility."

Yes. Young. He's young. I shake my head to rid myself of the image of Peter, freshly scrubbed and hatless, singing softly to his baby daughter.

"How about you?" Daniel asks. "Do you go to school?"

"Not anymore," I say. "I left when my brother...I'm going to be looking for work in the Soo." We're both quiet for a moment, the silence growing larger around us.

"Do you like poetry?" he asks, breaking the spell. "I could recite."

I cringe. The last thing I need right now is poetry. The last thing I need right now is to think about Jonathan.

"I don't have to," he says. "I just thought...well, I thought it might help pass the time, keep our minds busy...keep our spirits up. We have a great teacher up on the island. He got a few of us to keep studying. Reading, reciting, discussions. We'd come in after helping our parents out on the farm or the shop or on the water. I'm no scholar, but I like to read. It will help keep us both awake. I'll recite a poem."

"Okay. You're right. Go ahead. Just no rhyming ones, okay?" I make a laughing noise that I hope sounds like I'm teasing.

"Hmm...let me think..."

I lean down to check on my cousin again. He hasn't spoken since he sang the hymn. His eyes are closed still, but the captain is now staring into the distance as if observing something on a stage. I pat his hand and he moans, then chokes on his shallow breath like someone with a chest cold. I withdraw and place my palm on Peter's chest. Nothing. No movement. No warmth. I hold the back of my hand in front of his mouth to see if I can feel any breath. My head is close to his, hair flying about in the wind, when I feel a tug. A firm, sharp tug. I pull back, but Peter's hand is in my hair, yanking me toward his face. His eyes bulge open. He gasps. His breath is hot against my face. I try to pull away, but he's surprisingly strong for a man who hasn't moved in hours. I can hear the rattle of his inhale, the gurgling in his throat.

"I know, I know. What about 'Kubla Khan'? By Coleridge?" asks Daniel.

"Is that you, Christina? Cousin?" Peter croaks, his voice barely more than a whisper, fingers still grasping my hair.

I try to keep my voice steady. "It is, Peter. It is."

"Tell Mary I love her. Tell her I tried. You know I tried."

His grip is fierce, as if clinging to life itself. "You can tell her, Peter," I whisper. "You'll be all right. You will. You'll see. We're close to land. We'll get you back to Mary."

"Tell her, Chris. Promise." His voice is quiet, but firm, undeniable.

"I promise. We'll tell her together. You saved my life, cousin."

"Do you know it? Christina? 'Kubla Khan'? It's a wonderful poem. Maybe a bit old-fashioned," Daniel calls, unaware of what's happening at the other end of the boat. "Mad, yes, written when Coleridge was in an opium-induced haze, I've been told, but beautiful all the same. I memorized it last year."

I stop trying to resist Peter's pull and lean over to kiss his damp, cool forehead. When I lift up, I see his eyes are shut again. We are nearly nose to nose. I can't feel any life in him at all.

"No!" I say. "You can't go! I won't let you."

"Christina? Are you okay?" Daniel calls.

I put my head down on Peter's chest, my ear to his heart. There is nothing there now, no sound at all. My own heart is beating wildly, as if to make up for my cousin's. I try to pull away again, but my hair is wrapped tightly in his fingers. I can't bear to speak, can't bear to break this bond, and yet I can't stay in his death grip forever.

The captain glances over at me absently, as if waking from a dream, and I try to telegraph to him that I need help. *Help me*, I say to myself, over and over. "Help me," I manage to rasp aloud.

I watch the captain take us in, his eyes barely focused, lips dusky and dark. Slowly, with great effort, he rolls himself sideways and lifts a heavy hand to his first mate's wrist. He tugs my cousin's fingers free of my hair, then flops back with a groan.

I pull myself to sitting, try to collect myself. I can hear the captain breathing loudly, the sound like the growl of a frightened animal. He moans, "Ohhhh," then does it again. I reach down and place my open palm on his wide barrel chest. "It's going to be all right, Captain Savage. We're going home." I hold my hand there for a few minutes, trying to offer comfort, though there is little to give. I keep it there as his breath slows, then stops altogether.

"Christina? Are you okay? What's going on? I can hear you talking but not the words. Did something happen? What's going on?"

I glance back and forth between the two men lying shoulder to shoulder. The captain's jaw is slack, mouth agape. All of them are gone. The men in suits, the cabin boy and now the captain and Peter. Daniel and I are alone.

I look up and see the sky is inky black, not even a flicker of light. We have been abandoned by the stars and moon as well.

Six

"Daniel?" I call, trying to keep the desperation from my voice. This night will never end. At home I sometimes wake up from a dream trying to shout but no sound comes from my mouth. Here, in this waking nightmare, screaming won't do any good. Nothing will help us. Daniel has been silent since I told him that the captain and my cousin died. He seems to have forgotten all about his earlier plea for us to keep talking.

"Are you awake?" I ask.

"Uh-hmm," Daniel mumbles from far away.

Maybe it's his sluggishness or the fact that every other person in the boat is dead, but I don't care anymore what Daniel and his uncle were fighting about. I don't care if he's a pickpocket or a bank robber. What could he do that would be worse than what is happening right here, right now? In fact, I don't feel afraid of anything.

"Why don't you come sit with me?" I ask before I can really consider what I'm saying, before I can think through if we can even keep the boat balanced that way. But at least he'll have to stand up—he'll have to move. And having him here beside me will keep my mind from wandering to the men lying dead at my feet.

I have been trying not to look at them, trying not to think how Peter died with his fingers twisted in my hair. But my eyes drift there unbidden. I can't help feeling Daniel and I are like some smaller, weaker versions of the ferryman of Hades in the ancient myths and poems Jonathan loved. This ancient man would take the dead across the River Styx in his boat. If you didn't pay him the coin he was due, you'd have to wander the bank of the river for a hundred years. What would these dead men think of the fact that we are not rowing at all but letting the wind take us where it will? What would they think of their lame ferrymen, too cold and terrorized and hungry to steer?

"I can't," Daniel says, so much later that I can't even remember what he's talking about. "I want to keep the boat steady. I should stay"—he swallows, and even from the other end of the boat I can hear the smack of his tongue against the roof of his mouth—"here." The effort to say these few words has depleted him. His breath is shallow, ragged, in the stillness.

"Are you all right?" I ask.

He groans.

"Are you injured?"

Daniel still doesn't say anything. I listen hard for a response. Even another groan would give me hope. I don't know what I'll do if I'm the last one alive. The knowledge that there is another living person in this boat is the only thing keeping me upright. I wait a few more minutes, but Daniel says nothing.

I have to find out if he's all right. I have to wake him up if he's gone to sleep. I can't lose him too.

I can barely see my hand in front of my face, but I know vaguely where the bodies are, and I place my boots carefully as I make my way to the other end of the lifeboat. Once, I feel something soft give beneath my toe and lift up quickly, horrified that I've stepped on someone. I grab the gunwale, and the boat rocks but returns quickly to even keel.

I forget to breathe. If Daniel is dead I will lose my mind like that woman Jonathan and I once saw outside the Toronto Lunatic Asylum. We were out for a long, slow walk to help clear his lungs and ended up lost not far from the asylum. With its high brick walls, it looks more like a prison than a hospital. The woman was being led by the arm along the wall. She had messy, unkempt hair, no hat and an ill-fitting dress. She was talking loudly about nonsense. The man with her clutched her fiercely, refusing to look at anyone passing them, as if both protecting her and protecting the other people on the sidewalk from her. We tried not to stare. But the two of us talked about this encounter for months. There was something about the woman's ferocious presence, her insistence on those nonsense words, her determination to be heard, that seared itself into my mind.

I can sense the sides of the boat narrowing as I move toward the stern. I pause to take a deep breath. "Daniel," I say quietly, not wanting to startle him. "Daniel? Are you awake? You need to wake up."

He groans again. Relieved to hear any sound at all, I keep talking. "It's not a good idea to sleep. You said so yourself. We have to help one another."

I reach out to touch him, and in the darkness my hand lands on his. Before I can pull away, he squeezes. His grip is surprisingly strong, like Peter's fingers in my hair. I resist the temptation to pull away and sit down beside him holding his hand. Something in this touch spreads through my body like heat, traveling up my arm, across my shoulders and down my torso. I squeeze back and look at him.

We're so close, I can just make out his face, his eyes closed, his mouth soft. He startles as if he wants to say something but instead sighs and sinks farther sideways. We stay like that. I imagine I'm sending him what little reserve of strength I have left. I imagine we are beneath a heavy quilt, a fireplace blasting its warmth toward us. I'm drifting to sleep in this comfortable dream.

No. I have to fight the pull of sleep—I have to fight the sweet relief of letting go. I roll my head from side to side, pinch myself with my free hand. I'm not sure if my eyes have adjusted to the darkness or if it's getting lighter, but I can see Daniel more clearly now. He's slumped forward like a drunk outside a hotel, chin on his chest. His hand is heavy in mine, and I'm swamped with dread.

"Daniel," I say, pulling my hand away and grasping both his shoulders. "Daniel?" He is loose, sagging, like a canvas sail emptied of wind.

I shake him again, and he opens his eyes, staring at me in surprise, as if he's never seen me before and can't imagine why a stranger would have her face so close to his. I want to shout for happiness that he is alive. I can feel my mouth stretch into a smile like a ridiculous clown's. Daniel gamely makes an effort to grin back before closing his eyes again.

"You can't sleep! I won't let you," I say. Our faces are so close I can feel his faint breath on my cheek.

"I'm not going to leave," I say. "Not until you open your eyes."

But Daniel shifts away from me on the bench. He stiffens. He isn't grinning anymore. He speaks in a croaky whisper. "You have to go. You must." He raises his voice. "Go!"

I'm surprised by the effort it takes him to say this, but I'm not going anywhere. I'm not going to let him die. The wind has eased, and there's little risk of flipping. I will keep him clinging to life by the sheer force of my will.

"I'll go here," I say, moving to the next bench. "But I'm staying with you. I don't think you should sleep."

Daniel groans.

"I really don't think you should sleep."

But Daniel seems to be growing dimmer, a light flickering out. Is this how people slip from life? Their body less clear, the outline of their self fading into the air, the sky? I didn't notice with the others—I didn't even see my own brother die. I couldn't bear it. Mother called me in after he was gone, and I kissed his cool hands, his smooth forehead.

I can make out Daniel opening one eye, then the other. He looks sleepy and confused, like a child woken from a nap, and I have the urge to pull him close. I can't lose him. Not now. I'm about to start singing scales—anything to keep him awake—when he finally speaks.

"I'm awake." he mumbles. "Are you happy?"

"Well," I say, "I'm not sure I'd say *happy*. But you're not going to die on my watch."

Daniel leans to the side, struggling to prop himself up further. He goes in and out of my line of vision, and I rub my eyes.

"I think I'll sing," I say, but as I'm about to open my mouth, I realize I can't see his face at all now. I'm barely a foot and a half away from him. I blink hard once, then twice, trying to focus. I still can't see him. He's gone. Disappeared.

"Daniel?" I say tentatively, my heart in my throat.

"Hmmm?" he says, the sound coming from exactly where it was before.

"I can't see you. Can you see me? I thought…I thought you were gone. Where are you?" I reach out my hand. My hand seems to disappear as well, but I touch him. His shoulder. I think.

"It's like we're in a dream," I say. "Like we've drifted into a cloud."

"Fog?" he says weakly.

Fog? Of course. I look around the boat and can't see anything. We are completely socked in. I've never seen it so thick. When I was little, I imagined heaven like this. Clouds everywhere, all the edges rubbed away, though it was always brighter—even sunshiny somehow. I haven't thought about such things for ages. I haven't thought about heaven or hell at all except to ask, *What kind of god lets someone like my brother die?* He was a better person than I will ever be. He looked after everyone. People in our family. Children with no other friends. The ones who smelled bad or were overly interested in something like steam engines or insects. The ones whose parents made them work all the time or who beat them. Ally and I called these poor souls Jonathan's strays. He was kind to them all. Why did he die, but I survived? There is nothing right, nothing fair about it.

I have railed against this injustice so many times these last months, fearing at first that I would be struck down by a thunderbolt like Zeus does so often in Jonathan's myths. Then I grew more bold, throwing my questions into the wind, speaking aloud of my disappointment and fury with such a cruel god. Mother slapped me across the face when I said it to her.

"Christina?" Daniel's voice cuts through the fog.

"Sorry. It's fog. You're right. It's just fog."

"I'm not going to die, if that's what you're worried about..." He chokes, breathes deeply. "I'm just tired. And cold. Talking takes away my breath. I'm trying to conserve my strength."

"Okay," I say.

"Come sit with me again," he says. "Please?"

I don't hesitate. I squeeze in beside him, not thinking about anything but this minute. Even after everything that's happened, after everything I've done up to now—the running away, the anger—I think my mother would be most appalled by my sitting here so close to a strange boy. Even Ally would be shocked. We aren't allowed to be alone in a room with boys our age, never mind shoulder to shoulder. But there is nothing normal about this situation. Surely such rules don't apply.

Neither of us speaks. There is nothing to say. I listen to his breath. The longer we sit, the deeper and louder it gets. I fall inside its rhythms, warmed by his closeness.

"I'm scared," he says eventually.

"Me too," I say. "I'm scared too." And without thinking, *purposefully* not thinking, I reach toward him. His hand is right there, and we clasp each other, fingers sliding between fingers.

"And...and I feel responsible...I should have helped more, saved people," he says. "Some of them were clinging to me because I had a life preserver. They were drowning, and they nearly drowned me. I pushed them off. I pushed them away." He's speaking slowly, methodically, as if he's been thinking about this the whole time we've been in the boat. "I had to save myself..."

I'm about to interrupt, to reassure him that anyone would have done the same, that no one could blame him, but something in his voice stops me.

"I knew...I knew myself more in that moment than I ever have before," he says. "I knew I would do anything to survive. Anything." He pauses. Gulps.

"Now all I can think about is why it should be me who survives and not the others. Why me?"

It's strange to hear such words from someone else. I bite the inside of my cheek to keep from crying. The fog is still thick enough that I can't see Daniel's face clearly despite being so close. His breathing has changed again, as if saying this out loud has taken something from him. I know I should offer comforting words, but all I can do is squeeze his hand.

"There!" Daniel shouts and pulls his fingers from mine, twisting around in his seat. "A light! Do you see it?"

I look where he's pointing, then everywhere else. I can't see anything.

Daniel jumps to his feet with more energy than he's had in hours, and the boat rocks. "Careful!" I cry out, gripping the gunwales to steady us.

"It's there," he says again, sitting down slowly. "I swear I saw it." His voice is quieter now, as if he doesn't even believe it himself.

The wind is picking up, though it's warm compared to the water. We're drifting more quickly, and the breeze begins to push the fog. It remains thick, but I can at least see Daniel now, his pale skin, tousled hair, his wrinkled jacket hanging loose on his shoulders. He's a shadow of the boy I saw storming down the walkway back on the *Asia*, the boy who swam toward our lifeboat with so much determination that no one could turn him away.

He sighs, his head slumping to his chest again. He's probably thinking, as I am, of Mr. Sullivan, who only a few hours ago claimed to see a light from shore just before he died.

I squint into the fog, searching, hoping Daniel is not going mad, that he's not dying, that I'm not. But I see nothing.

"Tell me more about the store," I say. "Just keep talking. If the light is there, it's not going anywhere. I'll see it. Just talk to me. What are your plans? Is it a big place?"

But Daniel isn't going to be jollied. "I think you should go now," he says. "I'm going to try to use the oar."

"Are you sure? You don't look well. Maybe paddling isn't a good idea this minute. You said it yourself. It's going to be hard with just one oar, and it's so big. Maybe you should rest." I'm babbling now. I barely know what I'm saying. "We can wait until there's more light in the sky, till the fog is gone.

We'll know more then, maybe be able to figure out where we are, where we should try to go."

"I'm sure," he says, an edge to his voice. He gestures with his chin for me to head to the bow.

"But…" I say, searching his face. I don't know what's going on, what's changed.

"Go," he says firmly.

I stand up. It wasn't so long ago that Daniel was groaning, his head lolling off to the side. I watch him, but he's not looking at me. He stares intently toward the place he saw the light.

"I think it's Byng Inlet," he says as I'm moving away. "There's a light there. We've been drifting in that direction. I'm certain of it."

I try not to look down as I negotiate the bodies of the dead men but can't help catching glimpses of pale faces, tangled limbs. I tuck into my old spot on the floor at the bow. It's cold and damp all alone. I put my hands under my armpits to keep warm and puzzle over why Daniel turned on me like a sudden storm. Should I have lied and said I saw the light just to keep his spirits up? I don't know anything anymore.

"You think we can get there—Byng Inlet—if we paddle?" I call to Daniel in the loudest voice I can manage. A peace offering.

"Well," he calls back to me, "since we have just one oar, and we're both cold and exhausted…and since we haven't hit land *yet*, I'd say odds are…we'll freeze to death or die of exposure like the others if we do nothing."

I shrink into the floor of the lifeboat. Daniel's voice reminds me of his uncle on the boat, his cruelty unleashed.

I turn to hide my face, my quivering mouth. I can barely see Daniel, and I hope he can't see me. I tuck my legs into my chest, rest my chin on my knees and try to rub my legs with my hands to keep my blood circulating. My feet are heavy wooden blocks, wet and cold and unmanageable.

The boat rocks as Daniel starts paddling. It feels like I'm leaving my stomach behind each time we move. The oar frequently hits the side of the boat, and the whole vessel shudders. He pauses after a short while, and we continue to glide.

"We'll reach land," he calls out, as if regretting his sharp words. "We have to."

"Yeah," I say, looking around at the darkness. "We have to."

The movement of the boat through the water—the slap and splash—is a kind of conversation. I force myself not to think about why Daniel got so irritated or about his hallucination of a light. I try not to think about anything. And yet my mind strays to where it always seems to go in quiet moments: Jonathan.

All our lives, people asked us what it was like to have a twin. That was after they got over the obvious—I'm a girl and he's a boy, and we don't look anything alike. He's tall and I'm not. He has straight blond hair, and I have long dark curls. He has lots of friends and seems to gather people around him like a mother hen. I have one friend—Ally. And Jonathan. Jonathan, of course.

When we were small, the two of us had a secret language. It was just sounds and gestures, but we got our message across to each other. I don't remember the details, just the happy, contented feeling of having another person understand me, know me, in a way that I will probably never feel again. We stopped one day because Jonathan told me Mother didn't like it. We were still little. I hadn't noticed anything, of course. But he said he could tell she felt left out. He couldn't bear to make anyone feel bad.

I've heard people say that when someone they love dies, they learn more about themselves, that they grow up somehow, even if they're already adults. People even said it to me, as if it was something commonplace I should expect, like change from a quarter when you buy a newspaper on the street. They claimed death teaches a person something important about living. But the only thing I've learned through all of this, all this suffering, is that life is unfair.

It's hardly a wonder my parents wanted to send me off to work. It's hard to be around me. I'm an open wound. A gash that won't heal. I'm sure there are some families who pull together in times of crisis, but we weren't like that. None of us can talk about it. Jonathan was the center of our family, the beating heart around which all else circulated. All goodwill and kindness we showed one another emanated from him. Now we are stranded, trying to preserve ourselves but unable to preserve each other. Mother and Father hardly acknowledge one another except to pass the salt, to collect the milk.

The only person I could even bear to be around these last few months was Ally, though I've pushed her away now too. She loved Jonathan as I did. When we were children, we would have elaborate marriage ceremonies for the two of them. I would wind her up in a white sheet, a doily on her face for a veil. He would pluck some flowers from the garden behind our house for her posy. I was the minister, and I went on and on in the kind of rising and falling voice I'd heard so many times from the pulpit. When I said he could kiss the bride, Ally would dissolve into laughter, sputtering and chortling so hard that she fell down. Later, she still loved him, though he was too busy being, well, being Jonathan, helping everyone, being kind to wounded creatures. I don't know what would have happened if he hadn't become ill, if he had been allowed to grow up. I don't know if they would have married, but I know she has suffered as I have since he died.

I hear Daniel groan. I can see him now clear as day, the fog about two feet off the water. He's on his belly, leaning over the side of the boat, the oar still in the water. He turns his head to me. "Shallow," he says, without the urgency the word seems to require. "It's getting shallow."

And before I even have a chance to look over, water splashes me, then pours off my face like a waterfall. There's a loud crunch, the unnerving sound of metal grinding against rock. Daniel falls back into the boat as we abruptly stop moving.

"Land!" Daniel says, leaping to his feet. "It's land." His eyes burn with the fervor of a believer.

The sun is emerging from the distant horizon, and I can begin to see around us. It doesn't look like we're anywhere near land, though we are unmistakably stopped. There is nothing but water everywhere, small waves producing whitecaps and foamy spray.

It must be a shoal. An underwater rock. Discovering that I was correct about this possibility offers me no pleasure. We're grounded.

On that summer trip up to the Soo a few years ago, I remember thinking the entire eastern shore north of Parry

Sound must be guarded by an underwater rock fortress. Some of the shoals near the outer islands looked smooth and rounded, like a bald man's head popping up above the waterline. Others were deep, just yellow and greenish shapes shifting beneath the surface of the water. And there were those, like the one we must be sitting on right now, hidden just below. If you know the area, you might be able to pick your way through in a small sailboat or a dinghy, but in anything bigger, one wrong turn and you'll surely hit something. It's no wonder so many ships are lost out here.

Or maybe I'm the one who's delirious this time. Maybe we *have* reached land. I squeeze my eyes closed, then open them. I still see nothing but blue.

"I don't see it. The land," I call reluctantly to Daniel. "What is it?"

"Not sure," he says, excited, his cheeks flushed pink. The boat heels wildly as he leans over the side, then sits up straight again. He slips off his shoes, takes a deep breath and swings one leg over the gunwale. We rock back and forth. There's a rush of air to my mind, clearing away all the haziness of hunger and fear as he throws his other leg over the side and disappears.

Seven

This can't be happening. It isn't happening. Cold water splashes onto my face again, forcing me to focus.

"What are you doing?" I shout, extending my hands wide to steady the boat. When I raise my voice, I realize, with a flinch, that all this time I have been worried about speaking loudly for fear I would wake up the others in the boat. The dead people. I have been worried that I will wake the dead. None of this makes any sense.

"Daniel? Daniel?" I shout, terrified to move too much to one side in case he grabs on and we flip the lifeboat. In a second, maybe two, there's splashing, and I see his head pop up right beside me. He spits water from his mouth and flings his head to the side to get the hair from his eyes.

I'm not sure if I'm more angry or relieved. "What are you doing?"

Daniel doesn't answer. Instead he swims easily around the boat, as if he weren't practically dead a few minutes ago, as if a refreshing plunge in the freezing Georgian Bay water is exactly what he needed. He seems to be looking for something. I track his head and splashing arms like a hawk tracks a field mouse, terrified that if I look away, he'll disappear into the black, black lake.

Then I do lose sight of him, and it occurs to me that I'm going to have to jump in myself to rescue him. But he emerges on the opposite side of the boat. "Get the oar," he says.

I can see it propped up against the inside of the boat, handle in the air, near where he was using it. My stomach clenches. I'll have to navigate the dead men again. I steel myself, gripping the gunwales fiercely.

Daniel pulls himself up on the side, and I instinctively lean in the opposite direction. He's heavier than me, and I can't compensate for him entirely. I stumble and bang my hip against a metal grommet.

"We're stuck on a rock," he says. "But it's not too bad. We weren't going fast."

He drops off the side again and seems to be inspecting the hull underwater. I lurch toward the stern, eyes narrowed, to get the oar.

"What do you want me to do?" I ask when he resurfaces, though I'm still uncertain if he's brave, insane or both.

Slowly Daniel drags himself up to standing on the shoal. He shivers visibly when the wind hits his wet clothes and skin. The water comes up to just under his knees.

"I'll push and lift while you pry with the oar," he says, breathing heavily. "We have to do this carefully, or it could make any damage worse."

I don't entirely understand his plan, but he's not waiting. He stands on the rock near the stern and directs me toward the middle of the boat. He shows me where to push against the submerged rock with the oar while he lifts. Then, without pausing, he leans down, bending his knees to get a better angle. I can see his feet slipping slightly on the rock.

It's hard to imagine he'll be able to lift a metal boat with six people in it, even with me working the oar. Not today. Probably never. Still, I don't have a better idea. I wait for his nod.

"Now!" he says, shaking with the effort. The oar slips a bit on the algae-covered rock, then catches on a crack. I lean in with all my weight and feel the boat budge a little.

We rest for a second. "Again," he says. I inhale deeply and lean on the oar. This time we don't move at all.

"Are you sure?" I ask. "Maybe this isn't a good idea. If the shoal punctured the boat, it's the only thing keeping us from taking on more water. We'll sink. We could wait. We could wait for the sun to come up more."

But Daniel just shakes his head. "Ready?" he asks.

What else am I going to do? Fight him? Besides, I'm too bewildered to argue. "Ready," I say unconvincingly.

This time Daniel grunts loudly as he tries to lift the boat. My oar keeps slipping on the rock, but then I feel it slide into a ledge, and I can really lean in. We move the boat another few inches. We're both breathing heavily when we take a break.

"You all right? Can you do it again?" he asks.

"Just a minute. I need to catch my breath."

"Okay, but it's kind of cold here," he says.

"Sorry. I just need to take off this life preserver."

"Just a few more pushes, and I think we'll get it."

I nod, slipping off the heavy vest.

"Okay?" he says. "Ready? One, two, three, heave *hoooo…*"

I see Daniel's face redden, and I push off, leaning hard, putting everything I have into it. Daniel's lifting and leaning too—he's nearly horizontal, his head practically level with the gunwales. At first we get nowhere. Then suddenly the boat comes loose and slides off the rock, swinging out to the right because of my prying. As the boat moves, Daniel loses his footing on the slippery shoal and falls forward. He grunts as he hits his head on the metal hull. Hard. He falls into the water with a splash.

"Daniel!" I drop the oar inside the boat and scramble to get close to him. He's lying face-first in the water, motionless. I grip the fabric of his jacket and yank on his shoulder to try to flip him over. He's heavier than he looks. How long can he go without breathing? I can feel bones through his clothes.

The boat is heeling so much that I'm practically in the water myself, but I manage to flip him partway over, then all the way. His legs are hanging down into the greenish depths, but his chest is buoyant. That's got to be a good sign. He has air in there. I don't look straight at his face, afraid of what I'll see. I know there's blood. Lots of it.

I have to get him back in the boat. But my arms are jelly, and my shoulders ache. I'm not sure I can help him, but I have to try. I think of that woman in the stateroom next to mine. The little children I didn't save.

I wedge my left foot against the bench in front of me and lean over, grasping Daniel under the armpits to try to drag him over the gunwales. I manage to get both of his arms up, but water is pouring into the boat, splashing onto the dead men.

My foot slips, and I lose my grip. I let him go and brace myself so I don't fall in too.

Daniel is sinking—his chin is submerged. It's going to have to be all in one shot. Now. I take a deep breath, lean over and grab him under the armpits again. I yank up and lean back. I've got his head and torso out of the water. But I'm losing my hold. He's heavier out of the water—slippery too. I don't know how I will get him over the edge without breaking his back or my own.

I close my eyes, take a deep breath and release a kind of primal roar as I give one final heave up and in. I've got his torso, hips, his rear. He slips over the gunwale and crumples on top of me inside the boat, lower legs and feet still dangling over the side.

I lie silently for a moment, staring at the brightening sky, my heart thundering in my throat. The sky is pinkish around the edges, pale blue in the middle. It looks enormous, like a giant glass garden cloche. It would be beautiful if it weren't for the fact that I'm surrounded by dead men, pinned to the floor of the lifeboat by a bloody, soaking wet, apparently unconscious boy.

At least he's breathing. He coughed once after he landed on me. And I can feel his chest moving up and down. But he's out cold. Heavy as a gravestone. I slide out from underneath, careful to cushion his head from hitting the metal boat, turn his face to the side and prop him on my life preserver. I flip his legs and feet into the boat and maneuver myself to sitting.

It's worse than I thought. He has a gash on his left temple that's streaming blood. The area all around it is raised and bruised, a purple sunrise. The water at the bottom of the boat has turned crimson. I look around for something to use to apply pressure to his wound, but there's nothing clean or dry. My skirt is too wet for the fabric to rip. One of the men probably has a handkerchief in his pocket. The thought of touching them makes my stomach heave, but Daniel can't afford for me to be squeamish. I lean over the bench and open Mr. Sullivan's jacket. I try not to touch him, though my hand brushes against his chest. I force myself not to see his dark mustache, his rigid pose, his deadness.

I'm lucky. There's a clean handkerchief in the inside pocket, and I gingerly fish it out. It's wet but still pressed and folded, unused, a small square with his initials embroidered in the corner.

I press the cotton to Daniel's wound. It's immediately soaked in blood. The raised skin around the cut is spongy, swollen. I fold the handkerchief over a few times and hold it there firmly, looking away.

The horizon is a thin line dividing the water from the sky. I try to concentrate on it. On its solidity. Other people in the world can see it too. I am not alone under this big blue dome.

The surface of the water is like crumpled bedsheets, all ripples and folds. I can't see any more shoals, though they must be here. What if we hit again? How will I do this on my own? The boat bobs gently to the rhythm of the wind. It's completely silent, and I am suddenly more tired than I have ever been in my life.

I hadn't noticed before, but in the silence I realize that the wind had filled my head with noise. Even when no one was shouting at me or talking or singing, there was a din. A constant, unrelenting din. But now there is nothing, not a sound except water lapping against the broadside of the boat.

I have always hated it in poems or books when the weather matches the mood of the characters or, more often, the melancholy narrator—*dark clouds hovered* and all that. It has always seemed so false to me, sentimental, put on. Yet this too—the gentle wind, the friendly pink sky—seems horribly wrong in such a desperate time. I shake my head. I really must be losing my mind now, contemplating poetry while Daniel bleeds to death.

I lift the cloth to inspect his wound. Blood leaks out, but it's no longer gushing. I keep pressure on it but again look away.

One summer a few years before the consumption, Jonathan got a horrible gash on his forehead when we were visiting our cousins in Owen Sound. He dove wildly into the water, full of good faith or reckless abandon, depending on who's telling the story, and he hit his head on something. Luckily, he didn't pass out and came up right away. But the blood was unreal, a veritable eruption, pouring down his wet chest and pooling at his feet. All of us were terrified, but he was completely fine. The bleeding stopped quickly, and we dove down again and again that day, trying to figure out what he had hit.

Daniel hasn't opened his eyes—he's not completely fine— but he's not bleeding as heavily anymore. "Daniel?" I say. "Daniel? Are you awake?"

He's limp, unresponsive. My legs are cramping, and I'm going to have to move. I smooth out Daniel's jacket, then think to look in his own pocket for a handkerchief. I slide my hand inside his coat, surprised by the warmth of his body considering where he's been. I find a hanky and a book in his inner pocket. They're both waterlogged. A thin volume. *The Rime of the Ancient Mariner.* Coleridge again. I know this one. We had to read it in school. The tale of a man adrift at sea with a boatload of corpses.

What a strange boy to bring a book like this on a steamer journey. I tuck it back in his jacket, toss the other bloody handkerchief to the bottom of the boat and replace it with Daniel's own. I wipe up around the cut and can see that the skin near the wound is raw and swollen, but the actual injury is relatively small. There is no tension in his face, his dark hair tangled and wet against his forehead. He looks young, innocent. Tenderness for him sneaks up on me. I place my palm on his smooth forehead and stroke his hair back. While my hand is cupped there, his eyes flutter open, then closed.

Surprised, I gasp and pull away, but Daniel doesn't actually wake up. His lids open again, eyeballs rolling back in their sockets, exposing the whites at the bottom. Then he sighs and seems to settle into the floor of the boat, all effort vanquished from his body.

I don't know what to do, how to help. I can't bear the idea of being so completely useless, trapped in this lifeboat with nowhere to go. I *have* to do something. I can't just sit here waiting for him to die. Waiting to be the last one. The only one. But I'm so dizzy and hungry. Tired. There is nowhere to go. Nowhere but where I have gone so many times before.

❖ ❖ ❖

It was before everything. About this time of year, though it was warm. September, with the heat and burning-wood smell of August in the air. Jonathan's consumption was in remission after he'd spent time at a sanitarium north of the city. But he was still so thin, and he tired from the smallest exertion. Ally and I decided to take him on a picnic in High Park to cheer him up and give him a dose of country air. Doctor-approved.

It's not very far from Parkdale, though the large plot of land dotted with trees and meadows makes you feel like you're a hundred miles away from the horses and streetcars, the noise and muck of town. People picnic there a lot, whole families spread out on blankets, fishing in the pond, tramping in the woods. It's peaceful, reviving—so long as you stay off the private property that skirts the edges. That summer a park constable shot a boy dead when he trespassed by mistake on someone's farm. Everyone said the constable was a hothead, that he shouldn't have been allowed a gun at all, that he murdered the boy sure as the day is long. And he was eventually charged and convicted, sent to hang from the neck until he was dead. People have always said the High Park pond is haunted, but since the shooting there are some who insist on giving the whole place a wide berth.

None of us cared about all that. Jonathan's friend Robert had scouted out a spot well within park boundaries, close to the pond at the base of a small rise near the meadow. Jonathan could rest if he needed to, but he could also see everyone, and we could jump in the water if the feeling took us. There are lazy willows there, and we set up picnic cloths under their wide embrace. We brought blankets to keep Jonathan warm, and a wicker-basket lunch—thick-cut bread and slabs of ham, some lemonade, the first apples of the season, pickles, pie. It was a perfect spread, a perfect day. Jonathan even seemed to be breathing more easily, and there was color in his cheeks. He lay happily on a thick tartan blanket, reading and watching everyone as we threw a ball, and some of the boys went swimming. Ally rolled down her stockings and dipped her toes in the water.

And yet, and yet. This is the part I don't really like to think about but can't stop running through my head. The part where I said things I wish I hadn't. Where I wasn't as kind or generous or understanding as I could have been. As I wish I had been. Especially now.

Everyone else was up doing things. Robert was collecting stones. Ally was off for a walk with another girl in the tall grasses near the orchard. One of Jonathan's school friends was showing off his handstand on the muddy pond bottom. I stayed with my brother to keep him company on the picnic blanket, but he didn't want to just enjoy the perfect day. He wanted to talk about dying.

Death isn't something most people want to talk about. Certainly not with your sixteen-year-old twin brother who's been sick for more than a year. I tried to dissuade him, to get him to talk about better things, hopeful things, like how well he'd done on the exams he'd written and the beautiful day we were having on the edge of the pond in the late-summer heat. But he was fixated. Not in a dramatic way. He wasn't like that. Not self-pitying. He just wanted to talk about how it felt to know that death is near. He wanted to talk to me, I think, in order to make sense of it himself, and because he didn't want me to worry. He didn't want me to suffer for him.

He'd discovered something important, he explained, something that made him feel better. He said that even though he didn't want to go, and there was much to live for, he'd tried to find a way to exist without despair, knowing that he would die soon. He said he'd thought about it and thought about it more and found that when it came down to the end, nothing mattered except other people. Love for other people, and their love for him. There wasn't anything else.

I'm not proud of it, but I didn't exactly embrace his revelation. I teased him. I said he was moony. He was *dans la lune*, as the French-Canadian man who helps Mother with the gardens always says. I told him he must be sun-drunk or that perhaps the lemonade had gone off. I said maybe he was intoxicated with love. Did he have something he wanted to tell me about he and Ally? I made light of his words. I teased him until he told me to go away. Jonathan, who so rarely spoke harshly, dismissed me with one hand. *Leave me alone.* His words sharp as a clam shell. He never mentioned it again. Not even near the end when no one, not even me, could have denied that he was, in fact, going to die.

In my own defense, I suppose I just couldn't bear to hear it. I wasn't ready. I was still thinking he would recover. That he was invincible. That he would fight off the illness, that he would fight off death. I regret it, of course. I regret everything.

✧   ✧   ✧

Water slams the lifeboat, sending us rocking. I look down at Daniel. He's paler now, still asleep or unconscious, eyes shut but chest rising and falling. I lift up the handkerchief. The blood on the cotton is less vivid, the color of a rusty nail.

He lets out a gentle moan, and his forehead tenses.

I want to help him, but my arms are heavy tree trunks. I'm stiff as a plank, and yet the part of me that makes me *me*— my soul, my heart, whatever you want to call it—is lying like a floppy fish out of water on the bottom of the boat, gasping for air, for life.

I don't know where Jonathan's calmness came from, how he could feel so peaceful when dying young is wrong. Just wrong. There is nothing right about it. Nothing that makes any sense. Nothing that lends itself to cheerfulness, to poise, to love. Even now, face-to-face with the very real possibility of watching Daniel die, maybe even dying myself, I only feel tired and angry. I'm not ready. It seems like such a wicked twist, such a waste. I leave home so no one has to be reminded of what we've all lost, so no one has to be constantly thinking about Jonathan's death, only to die myself? When I ran away I was sure they would be glad to be rid of me, glad not to have to deal with my moods, my anger. But I know now, with the clarity of a cold, brittle morning, that my parents will not survive if I am lost too. And Ally. Ally will not recover either.

I need to pull myself together. It's too early for rescue boats, even if they knew where to look for us. It's too late in the season to expect someone to just happen by. With Daniel passed out, it's up to me to get us to shore. If we are going to have a chance, it's up to me.

The morning sky isn't pink anymore. It's yellow and white, washed out with stillness. The bay is calm. A bird high in the air squawks loudly, startling me. It does it again, shrill and high pitched, touching me somewhere below my breastbone. It gets louder and louder. I can feel it in my throat. Now the bird is floating on the wind about fifty feet in the air above us. It has a white underbelly and distinctive head, a wide wing-span, black brushed on the tips as if dipped in paint. A seagull.

My grandmother, my mother's mother, who came to Owen Sound from Ireland, a no-nonsense woman who had ten children and lost five of them to illnesses, always said she'd like to return in her next life as a gull. She said it with a laugh, knowing there were those who'd think such a senti-ment, even spoken in jest, was sacrilege, paganism. She didn't care. She thought she'd like to glide on the wind like that, to see the world from up high. She loved fishing and admired especially the seagull's ability to spot its prey in the water from miles in the air.

She would take us for a walk along the docks in Owen Sound in one of her old-fashioned black dresses with the big wide skirt. She'd point out a particular gull as if she knew it as well as her own children. *Watch this one*, she'd say proudly. *He always gets his man.* And the bird would go from gentle gliding on the wind to dive-bombing toward the water, beak first. A small splash, then up and out, into the air, a minnow or small perch wriggling in its beak. With its white head tilted just so, gullet open, it would swallow the fish whole. Then, with a flap or two of its wings, the bird was hunting again.

The seagull above me floats on the breeze. It seems to be making no effort whatsoever. It's gliding slightly faster than our boat is moving, but when it gets too far ahead, it flaps its wings once, twice, tilting a wing down to circle back. I start to wonder if the bird is watching me. Maybe my grandmother *has* returned as a gull. She's up there in the sky ensuring I'm safe, that I don't give up hope, that we make it to shore.

More madness. I shake my head as if I can liberate my mind with a good jiggle. I notice Daniel's mouth twitching.

"Daniel?" I whisper and put my hand in his. "Squeeze my fingers if you can hear me."

Nothing.

Hwah, hwah, hwah. The seagull is louder now. Insistent. I look up to see it diving toward our boat. It's vertical, beak first, coming fast. It looks as if it's going to smash right into me, and I instinctively cover my head with my free hand. I hold my breath, squeeze my eyes shut. I open them in time to see the bird expertly pull up and land gently on a small triangle of metal at the bow. It walks around slightly, picking up its feet and placing them just so before settling on its haunches, as if in a familiar chair.

The bird stares at me. It is brawny, thick in the neck, its breast downy. Its beak is yellow with a hint of orange at the bottom front. Its eyes are dark, pupils huge. The creature turns away.

I don't want to move too much in case I startle it. Despite its lack of interest in me, I'm grateful for the company. Even a disdainful bird will do.

The seagull tucks its head into its wing and nips at itself, like finally getting at an unreachable itch. Then it looks at me again, unblinking. It makes my eyes feel dry just watching it.

"I wish I had something to feed you," I say in a quiet voice.

The bird cocks its head to the side.

"A nice fish maybe?"

The bird stands up on its feet and shortens its neck, as if pondering my question.

"You'd like that? I wish I had something to eat myself." I realize I'm starving, the gnawing hole in my stomach suddenly vast and unfillable.

"I wish you could tell me where we are," I say, warming to this one-sided conversation. "How close we are to shore."

But the bird is done with me and our conversation. It launches itself into the air without even looking back. I hear its high-pitched screeching as it disappears into the distance.

I sigh and glance back at Daniel, trying to fight off despair. He's unchanged, though the blood on his forehead is now dry. I gaze around at the endless water and endless sky, the boat full of dead men. Far ahead to the right there's a thick, dark line like a thundercloud. I rub my eyes with my fists. We won't survive another storm. I try to breathe, try to prepare myself.

I'm going to get the oar and start paddling like Daniel did. This is how I can take charge, how I can still the rattle of anguish in my chest.

I make sure Daniel is in a safe position and move past him and the other men. I reach the oar, but it's so long and awkward I have no idea how I'm going to use it to paddle.

I don't even know if we've been drifting in the right direction all this time. I look around again, trying to be calm, reasonable, hoping that what I should do will become obvious.

I push my hair off my face and lean over, gripping the oar that's taller than me with two hands. Holding the wooden shaft toward the middle, I sweep the long blade through the water. The boat moves sideways. I lean to the other side and sweep again. The boat moves back the same way we've just come. We're hardly moving forward at all. I'll have to keep doing this exhausting motion, altering right then left, if we are going to make any headway at all. I take a deep breath and continue. Right, left, right, left. I dissolve into motion, not thinking about anything.

Eventually my arms tire, and my fingers are cold and wet. I have to stop. I search the horizon. The dark line in the distance is becoming clearer. It's smoky, jagged. But there's something coming clearer. A dark shape. There, and there. It's not a storm at all. It looks like trees.

Eight

The first time I ran away was right after Jonathan died. I was driven by something I can't really think of as belonging to me, something so deep inside it was like an instinct rather than a decision. I was an animal in self-preservation mode. Even now I don't entirely understand why I did it.

I kissed my brother's cold forehead and walked out of the house, not bothering to close the door. I walked down our street toward the water, past wagons and horses and carts headed into Parkdale loaded with the first spring harvest. I didn't stop when I reached the Grand Trunk tracks. I traced the rail line eastward toward Toronto, ignoring the whistle blowing of the engineers, the wild gestures of the men telling me to get out of the train yards. I passed the Central Prison and the cattle market, the abattoir with its metallic smell of blood and manure and death. I'd forgotten my hat, and I must have looked ridiculous, like that madwoman at the lunatic asylum, but I barely noticed other people. Near the slaughterhouse, the putrid smell infiltrating my nostrils, my head, my skin, I began to head north again along the edge of the ravine.

I slipped between birch trees, listening to the crunch of leaves beneath my boots, and disappeared down the slope into a shallow valley. There are a few houses dotted here and there up top, but at creekside I was all alone. The fresh scent of wet soil and rushing spring water reminded me of walks in the woods with my family, hunting for trilliums and fiddleheads we'd eat straight from the ground. I'd never been to that creek before, though I'd read about it. It was all over the newspapers. People crying foul because of the garbage thrown there. City engineers had been trying to straighten the unruly stream, dig in a sewer pipe. But where I walked, the banks were clear of debris and the sound of the water was comforting in its fury, so loud I couldn't hear my own grief.

Spring came late this year, and the creek was swollen, pushing water through to Lake Ontario, carving out the sandy riverbanks in its haste, digging at the roots of the oak and pine and birch trees growing there. I walked northward in the mud closest to the water, leaping from stones to roots to trees fallen over the narrow bed. The farther I went, the more garbage I saw—rusted-out cans and bones, unidentifiable metal, rotting leaves and muck.

I passed a school with its pointy spires and rushing students, gates and lawns, the tiny rooms crowded with books. From there the creek dove down deeper into the earth, until I could barely see the upper edge of the slope amid the tangle of trees and brush. The air felt cleaner. The city far away.

I've seen maps of Toronto where the many rivers that slice through it from north to south look like fractures in the land, or perhaps serpents, their curves and twists threatening the grid created by politicians and businessmen. Being down there beneath the city with its careful order, its rigid lines, I followed only the anarchy of the earth. Tangled and unruly, yet certain in its disorder. Every step I took seemed like confirmation of all that I'd felt through my brother's illness and death: that despite our urge to try to control every little thing, there is no such thing as control. We are only part of a much bigger something. What I wish for, what I hope, makes little difference to the world. The city might try to straighten out the river, try to build bridges over it, but the river will always win. It will flood or tear deeper into the earth. The houses on top will shift and fall inside. It sounds awful when I say it that way, but it's only awful if you fight it, if you try to control what is beyond control.

Walking through the ravine, the thought of giving up control made me feel strangely peaceful. The silence, the solitude, the embrace of the budding trees freed me. The impotent fury I'd been harboring throughout Jonathan's illness mixed together with the dirt and noise in a messy slurry. I surrendered it there on the banks of the creek, stamping my feet into the mud.

North of Dundas Street there was a fork in the river, and I headed west, down even deeper into the valley until the sides loomed over me and the city was completely erased from view. Pine and birch and oak trees leaned toward the creek. I came up near an apple orchard belonging to a huge home on the south bank of the river. Fields stretched north and west. The apple trees were gnarly and small, twisting this way and that like a many-armed creature. I sat down underneath one and stared at the sky, trying to make sense of the pieces of blue between the branches. I closed my eyes, and I think I fell asleep because when I woke the sun was lower in the sky, casting golden light over the orchard. I forced myself to stand up, to pound out the tingling in my feet. I remembered where I was, what had happened, and I started to walk again, counting footsteps to drown my thoughts.

❖   ❖   ❖

My arms are like frayed rope, my hands raw and bleeding again from handling the big wooden oar. I shake my head, stretch my jaw, twist my neck back and forth. Focus. I have to focus. The dark line on the horizon is growing more defined every minute. It's definitely trees. Lots of them. An island? The mainland? I don't care. Anything is better than being out here in the middle of the lake, going nowhere. I don't think I can survive another day at sea without food or something to keep me warm, to keep me from losing hope.

I lean into the oar, pulling the water one way, then the other.

Daniel is still unconscious. He hasn't moved while I've been paddling, though his breathing seems steady. If I had any lingering doubt before, it's gone now—getting us to shore is all on me. I'm going to have to do this on my own. If not for myself, then for him. If not for myself, then for the men I am ferrying to shore, for the relatives who will have a body, at least, to mourn.

I'm getting into a rhythm when I bang my elbow against the edge of the hull. My whole arm goes numb for a few seconds, and I forget to breathe. The pain is intense, shooting up to my shoulder. I curse out loud, and my mother's face is there in front of me as it was when I held Daniel's hand. Her pursed lips and disapproving face. I wonder at this power she has over me, simultaneously surprised that I have the wherewithal to wonder at all. Thinking about thinking has got to be a good sign. Paddling is making me feel alive again.

I put my head down and keep going. Despite my slow, awkward movement, the trees are getting closer. I'm sure of it.

For the first time in nearly a day, I'm warming up. Sweat dots my upper lip, and I lick it off. Salty. I rest the oar across the bow and glance back at Daniel. I try not to look at the others, their bodies lying twisted and broken on the floor of the lifeboat. I wish I could tell Daniel that I see land, that it's not hopeless. I wish I could tell him he was right.

He looks so young with his wet coat and trousers plastered to his skin, his hair slicked back from his forehead, the gash swollen and crusted over. It's hard to feel angry with him for trying to be a hero on that shoal. I remember what he said about his mother having a favorite, and I think how, despite her love for that other brother, she would surely mourn this boy with his poetry and impulsiveness.

I paddle and paddle and then rest again, my heart a hammer. My shoulders and arms are aching, and I finally rest the oar inside the boat and hang my head over the water. I watch the foam, little bubbles on the surface, ripples of wind, the forward motion of our boat.

I'm sitting up again, staring at Daniel, when I see his hand move. A quick flex of the fingers. I blink and it doesn't seem like he's moved at all. Until there it is again. I'm sure of it this time. He makes a fist with one hand, then the other.

"Daniel?" I call, getting into a better position. "Daniel, can you hear me?"

He whimpers. His eyes flutter and open. They are glassy, confused. He squeezes them shut again.

I look quickly toward the horizon. The trees are there but still far away. I can stop for a moment longer. I move to him, cup my hand over his, squeeze gently. He looks at me groggily, as if he's never seen me before. His pupils are huge, dark holes.

"Daniel."

His face is blank.

"It's Christina. Christina McBurney. We're in a lifeboat."

He blinks slowly. "Where am I?" he croaks when he opens his eyes again.

I take a deep breath and turn to look at the shore. I don't know where we are. We're headed for trees. That's all I know.

Daniel pulls his hand from underneath mine and tries to prop himself up.

"We're in a lifeboat," I say. "Our ship has been wrecked. We are...we are survivors..." I feel the word catch in my throat.

Daniel furrows his brow, still confused. "Who are you?"

My pounding heart sinks to my feet. He's worse off than he looks. "I'm Christina. Christina McBurney. You hit your head. You're going to be fine."

"Are you a doctor?"

"Uh...no..."

"Where's my uncle?"

I shake my head. "I don't know."

Daniel lies back down and looks away from me.

"We're in sight of land," I tell him. "I'm going to keep paddling toward it." What else can I do? It's surely better to be on solid ground. Even if no one else is there, I can help him better there.

Daniel doesn't even acknowledge me as I pick up the oar again, feeling the strain in my neck. Maybe he just needs a few minutes. He's in shock. It's like when you wake up in an unfamiliar bed and you're not sure where you are at first. The other possible reasons for his confusion are too awful to think about.

I put my head down and try to breathe normally. Stroke, stroke. I call out to Daniel that we're getting closer.

"It's going to be okay," I say, breathing heavily. I say it so many times, it becomes a kind of song in my head, more for me than anyone else. When I look up again I can make out a smooth rock sloping down to the water, a line of dark-green trees—cedar, pine—several hundred feet behind it.

"It's going to be all right," I call, halfway believing it for the first time. There seem to be big boulders in some parts, a low rock face in another. Mounds of smooth pink rock poke out of the water all around us. Some are smeared with bird poop, others are speckled, like black paint thrown at a pink canvas.

Daniel has his eyes open, but I'm not sure what he's taking in. He looks vacant, like an empty storefront. I push hair from my forehead. Sweat stings my eyes, tickles my cheek. I don't even bother to wipe it—I just blink hard and press my lips closed. *It's going to be all right.* It takes another half hour, but we get close enough for me to stop paddling and coast into shore. I put the oar in the boat, sit up, rubbing my neck, and watch the approaching land, searching for anything more than trees and rocks. The boat glides, then stops suddenly, grinding into the rock, wedged against something underwater. We're not going anywhere.

"Where are we?" Daniel asks. He raises himself up onto his elbows to look around.

"I don't know," I say. I pull my dress up at the bottom and heave myself over the side. I hop down, the wet rock right below me. My foot slips. I manage to grab the edge of the boat before falling, but I have to lean against the hull to hold myself upright and catch my breath again.

It's as if my legs are jelly. I can't control them. When I finally gather myself, I have to place each foot carefully on the rock, shifting my weight in order not to topple completely. My feet throb with pins and needles. I manage to get about ten feet before collapsing. The rock is warm compared to the air. I lie back and turn my head, pressing my cheek to the stone, and stretch out my crampy legs. I'm lying there when I see movement in the boat. Daniel is pulling himself up to sitting. He looks around, then down at the dead men, his mouth a crooked line.

"Let me help you," I call, hoisting myself upright.

"What?" He looks toward my voice, as if surprised anyone else is around. "No."

"Well, call if you need me," I say. I don't know what's going on with him, but I know I should look around. Maybe there will be fishing huts or a trapper's cabin. It's hard to tell if this is the mainland or a big island. Who knows how far we've come, but the sooner we figure it out and get Daniel to a doctor, the better. Darkness comes more quickly this time of year. We need to find food and shelter. We need to find help.

I glance down the shore, away from the boat. There's barely anything growing close to the water. A few clumps of low grass rise out of cracks in the rock. There's moss in the low-lying bits. The rock itself is not uniformly pink, as it looked from out in the water. It's cut through with swirling ribbons of black and white, gray and brown. There's a small deposit of a clear, crystal-like rock wedged into the stone right near where I'm sitting. It looks like a clutch of rough gemstones, sharp to the touch.

I stand up and test my legs again. They feel sturdier but are still stiff from the cold and lack of movement. It's a miracle, really, that despite being bruised and wet and exhausted, I'm not injured at all.

I begin to trace the shoreline to get a sense of where we are. I can still keep an eye on Daniel if I stick close to the water, and I won't have to go near the dense line of trees and the darkness behind it.

My feet ache as I negotiate the rocks. They're swollen and wet. I'd like to take off my boots, but I'd probably never get them on again.

The wind is starting to pick up. It's nothing like yesterday—not even close. The height and velocity of those waves seems almost ridiculous now, unbelievable, like an exaggerated version of reality. Looking out at the lake, all small, orderly tufts and gentle whitecaps, it is as if the bay is apologizing for its madness.

I don't make it very far before I have to stop and catch my breath. The sun is peeking out behind the wan clouds, and it warms me. It must be doing the same for Daniel because down the shore I can see him stirring in the lifeboat.

"Do you need help?" I call back.

"Is anyone here?" he asks.

"Nope. Just rocks and trees."

"Nothing else?"

"Not yet."

This is the most sense Daniel has made since he hit his head. I see him struggling to drag himself toward the side of the boat. But what if he falls when he gets out? Hits his head again? I pick up the bottom of my dress to run back. The forest is close to the water, and when I slow down to catch my breath I hear rustling in the bush. It's probably a squirrel or a bird. A creature unaccustomed to visitors. Still, I watch the bushes nervously as I take off again.

"I can hardly move," he says when I stop in front of him. "I feel like I've been run over by a train. We've been in the boat a long time."

I'm not sure if it's a statement or a question, but I answer anyway. "Yeah. I don't know how long—at least a day, maybe two. I lost track. Here, let me help you."

Daniel pauses for a second and lets me hold his arm as he slides over the side of the boat. He leans into me, but I stumble and my foot slips on the wet rock. It looks like we're going to fall in a heap, but he pulls back, and we stagger and regain our balance. We hobble together to a flattish part of the rock and flop down.

"I'm starting to remember," Daniel says, staring into the distance as if searching the horizon for his memories. "I remember you." He turns and offers a lopsided grin, then looks suddenly stern. "I remember the boat going down. My uncle screaming. Getting in the lifeboat and having it flip over. Again and again. People dying." He cringes. "But I can't remember why we survived. Are there others?"

"I don't think so. I don't know." I swallow. It's not going to be easy to tell this story to anyone, let alone the only other living person who's shared it with me. Maybe his memory of what's happened will be lost forever. It will only ever be my story. I'm hit with a wave of loneliness so powerful I feel like I'm drowning all over again.

"I held the lifeline that goes around the boat. You did the same," I offer. "That's what saved us. My cousin, the mate, told me to hold on and not let go. We were lucky..."

"The mate. Right." Daniel tilts his chin in the direction of the boat. "Now I remember. 'Pull for the shore, sailor'?"

"That's right. My cousin. Peter. You remember."

"Uh-hmmm...it's fuzzy. I still don't know how I hit my head. I have a goose egg the size of a dinner roll. A cut too."

"Yeah. I know. You should have seen the blood. Or not. Maybe not."

We are both silent for a moment.

Then I tell him about the shoal and how he banged his head trying to push us off. "It was scary," I say. "I thought you might not make it."

Daniel raises his eyebrows at this. "How did you get me back in the boat?"

"Yeah, that was hard." I shake my head.

Daniel feels the contours of the wound on his head. He grimaces. "Wow," he says shyly. "Thanks. So...what do we do now?"

I twist my lips, rub them together, trying to hide my surprise at this shift, his asking my advice, waiting for me to give instructions. "Well, we need to find food. And shelter. I don't know how much longer we can make it out here without something to eat.

"The weather can change in a blink," I add. "If it gets cold, we're...well, we're in trouble. I didn't walk far, but I can't see an end to this shore. Maybe someone will come by. Fishermen or trappers."

Daniel looks at me seriously and nods.

"We should take turns resting," I say. "The other can keep watch. Do you think you can stay awake? Be on the lookout?"

"Sure," he says, though he doesn't look sure of anything.

My arms are heavy, and my head is almost too much for my aching neck. That little burst of energy might be all I have. "Or maybe we should both rest."

"They'll be sending out search boats soon?" Daniel asks after a long silence.

I don't know what to say. Maybe he's more confused than he seems.

"They'll know something's wrong?" he insists.

"Well, I guess," I offer. "The telegraph was likely down in the storm. But if they don't know now, they will soon. People are waiting on the *Asia*. Boats will be sent out when it doesn't turn up. Someone will be searching. Soon, I'm sure."

"If we're near Parry Sound or Byng Inlet, maybe we could paddle," he says. "Along the inside channel."

I watch him speak, his face hopeful, searching mine for reassurance. And yet he's still frail, his skin pale. He looks as if he couldn't stand for more than thirty seconds. He didn't even recognize me not so long ago and remembers almost nothing of the last two days.

I don't know what to say. His innocence and neediness scare me. He has no idea what we're up against. The responsibility makes me feel impatient, itchy. I want to escape. It's what I do when I feel afraid. I run away, lash out. I'm not proud of it. In fact, I'm ashamed. And yet the words are out of my mouth before I can stop myself. "I saw you fighting with your uncle. On the ship. What was it about?"

Daniel scowls, as if there's a sharp pain in his head.

"I'm sorry," I say too late.

He doesn't speak, just keeps rubbing his eyes, as if luxuriating in it, as if it satisfies some profound need. He moves to his forehead, massaging it, careful not to put pressure on the wound.

Finally, when I'm starting to think he's forgotten my question like he forgot about the shoal, he asks, "What are you talking about?"

I sigh loudly, not certain what I've started, not certain I even care anymore. "I heard you," I say. "I heard you say you *wouldn't do it anymore*. You said something about police. And I saw you push him."

Daniel looks down at the rock gloomily, and I'm suddenly swamped with shame. Why am I badgering a boy with a head injury? Why can't I stop myself? "I'm sorry," I say again, but this time I mean it. I'm awful. "You don't have to tell me. You should rest. I don't know what...what—"

But Daniel responds before I can finish. "Push him? Seriously? Have you ever met my uncle? He's not the sort people go around pushing. I honestly don't know what you're talking about." Suddenly there's venom in his voice, that spark of fury I witnessed on the boat. "You're making it up. You're a liar."

I lean away. I guess this is what I wanted—to get a rise out of him. To force him out of his stupor. To make him stop thinking I am a person he can rely on. To arrest any notion that I will save us. But accusing me of lying?

I drag myself to standing and look down at Daniel, raising my voice louder than necessary considering our solitude, considering the fact that I started this in the first place. But it's like the plug has come out of the drain, as if all the tension of the last two days comes to a head in this moment.

"Are you serious?" I say. "Why would I lie about something like that?"

Daniel shrugs and looks down. "I dunno. Maybe you're crazy."

I probably do look insane with my hair unbound and blood staining the front of my dress. And I *am* the one standing, glowering, interrogating him when he's just emerged from unconsciousness. But I don't stop. I can't.

I practically spit out the words. "Maybe *you're* mad. Maybe you're the liar. I heard you on the boat talking about doing something criminal. How do I know you're not a thief? Or worse? How do I know you're not going to slit my throat right now?"

I take a few steps back, my own words throwing me off-balance. Daniel raises his eyebrows, then looks down at himself—his wet, bloodstained clothes, his body like a stick—and back up at me. He's broken, harmless.

And yet I'm too jumped up to slow the momentum of my emotions. I turn around and storm down the shore in the opposite direction. The wind is picking up now, and although my clothes are nearly dry, I shiver and hug my arms around my chest. I push away the voice in my head that begs me to turn back, to stop this stubborn, stupid game. Where am I going to go? What am I going to do? I'm starving, light-headed. Daniel and I have only each other to depend upon. And he's practically immobile.

Still, I keep walking. I'm a practiced denier, a walk-away-er. I've been running away for months now.

I use my hands to climb up a steepish rock face. There are barely any footholds, and I lose my grip, scraping my knee before catching myself, fingers like talons. The cut stings, but once I get up, I keep moving, focusing on the ground. Bright orange lichen carpets the rock. It looks like something splattered from a child's paint box, otherworldly on this harsh and inhospitable surface. Any plant that survives here must be resilient—able to withstand wind and rain and drought. They have to be fighters, opportunists, finding moisture in tiny cracks, crevasses, places where it looks like nothing could live.

Something about the triumph of these tiny plants makes my own struggle seem small, and my anger dissipates as I walk, like leaving a trail of clothes behind as you undress. I arrive at a place where boulders are strewn over a large area by the shore. I can't even see the lifeboat anymore.

A crayfish catches my eye, darting under a rock in the murky water. I lean down, try to get a better look, but it's gone. Crayfish and bass, bear and fox, beetles and snakes all have their own small worlds on this barren shore—their own fears and patterns, their needs and demands. There are people somewhere too. Fishermen and trappers and Indians. I might be alone right this minute, but I'm not alone altogether. I am still beneath the same sky, warmed by the same sun, my path lit by the same stars.

My body is starting to return to me. My feet feel more certain on the rocks, my arms less heavy and ungainly. I take a great big gulp of the air blowing off the lake. It smells a bit fishy, but it's cool, bracing, full of intent. Its job is clear: to blow away the cobwebs in my brain, blow away the cramps in my legs, the pain in my knees, the stubborn child in my actions. I have to stop acting like a hurt little girl. I need to put aside my pigheadness, my temper, my fear. I have to make sure we survive. Jonathan didn't, but I did.

I sit down on the rock and look out at the bay. I'm trying to gather my resolve, take in more of that cold, fresh wind, when a terrible *boom* cracks the air. It sounds like lightning, but the sky above is clear. There is nothing but low grass blowing in the wind, trees leaning this way and that. I hold my breath, listening, and then there's another, quieter *thud*, like something hitting the metal lifeboat. I start running and don't stop.

Nine

I'm sorry, I think with every stride. "I'm sorry," I say before I even see Daniel, before I have time to figure out if he's all right. My lungs are tight, breath coming out in short, sharp gasps.

The lifeboat is unchanged, but Daniel has moved. He's lying on another, more sheltered part of the gentle, rocky slope. He's on his back, eyes closed.

"Are you okay?" I call, quickening my pace.

He doesn't answer.

"Are you all right?" I try again when I'm nearly at his side. Up close, I can see his chest moving up and down. He moves his fingers in a feeble wave.

I sink to the rock beside him. He's still alive, still conscious. "What happened?"

Daniel is a bit sweaty. It must have taken a lot of effort for him to get here on his own. He's even taken off his jacket.

Except, I realize with a great heave of my stomach, it's not just his coat on the rock beside him. It's a body, face and torso covered.

I feel as if I'm back on the boat, pitching up and down in the waves. I can tell it's the cabin boy by the small, swollen hand poking out from beneath Daniel's jacket.

Daniel rolls his head toward me, eyes wide and unblinking. The sound I heard was probably him lifting the body out of the boat. No wonder he's out of breath.

"My head hurts," Daniel says eventually.

I nod.

"We need to get the rest of them out of the lifeboat," he says. "Bury them if we can. If we're going to paddle to Parry Sound with one oar, we'll need to be light."

The thought of touching the dead men, their cold flesh giving way beneath my fingers, makes my throat constrict. I try to position myself so I don't have to look at the cabin boy's thick fingers or his legs bent at an awkward angle. His trousers have ridden up, and I can see his calf, smooth and nearly hairless.

"Okay," I say, gulping back dread.

But neither of us moves for a long time. We stay on the rock without speaking, the wind banging the lifeboat gently against the shore.

When we finally begin our terrible task, I have to close my nostrils and breathe through my mouth again. The men are heaped in the bottom of the lifeboat like sacks of flour, faces pale, lips gray.

Daniel and I lift the captain out first. He's heavy, stiff, like he's been frozen solid. I take his feet, his boots scuffed and worn smooth on the bottom. Daniel carries his head and shoulders. We walk slowly, methodically, careful not to lose our grip. Daniel pauses often to close his eyes and breathe deeply. We lay the captain down gently on the rock near the cabin boy.

I return to the shore to rest a minute, but Daniel doesn't join me. Instead he moves quickly to a tangle of juniper bushes near the trees that guard the forest. I see him bend at the waist and retch loudly, over and over, his body shaking with the effort. I turn away and sing to myself to stop from throwing up too. When Daniel sits down nearby, I can make out the sound of him reciting a prayer under his breath.

Finally we get the others, grunting and sighing with the effort, moving slowly as if wading through deep water. My hands are freezing again, fingers stiff and inflexible. I become numb also to the shock of our task, unafraid to look at the dead men, to touch their cold skin. When we lay them down on the rock, I rearrange their clothing, carefully button their coats, pat down their hair. I say a small prayer for Mr. Sullivan's little boy. Before we lift Mr. McAllister out to join the others, I gently close the shoemaker's open eyes. "Rest," I say, as much for myself as for him.

My cousin is last. He looks so solitary in the lifeboat, small and pale amid the blood and water and cast-off life preservers and boots. But I refuse to think of him as discarded or alone. I think instead of my comrade of so many summers, a man whose wedding I attended, whose children I have held in my arms, whose care and quick thinking saved my life. I reach into his front pockets, search inside his coat, in case there's anything he might want me to give his family.

I find a small package wrapped in oilcloth. It's a damp sailor's logbook, a recent studio photograph of Mary and the children tucked into the front, the edges already worn away. I imagine Peter in his mate's berth at night, holding the photograph in his hands, worrying the corners. The backdrop is painted to look like an elegant parlor, a *trompe l'oeil* window of stained glass appearing to throw shadows on the ground. Mary is sitting upright in a velvet chair, the baby on her lap, their older son standing in front, his fat little hand resting on his mother's knee. The baby's face is soft, eyes wide and trusting.

"I'm sorry, Daniel," I say. "I just...I just need a minute."

I head to the water's edge, cup my hands and take a long drink. The water is perfectly cold, bracing against my sandpaper throat. I drink again and again just to feel the crystal clarity of the bay. I wipe my wet hands on my skirt and flip through the logbook again, admiring Peter's elegant handwriting but making little sense of the numbers and letters and lines inscribed there. I make sure the photo is safely stowed inside, rub my hands together for a minute to warm them, then undo a few buttons near the waist of my dress and slide the book inside.

We carry Peter to the rock where we've placed the others close together, as if they have all fallen sleep in a row.

"We should cover them so they're protected. From the wind—and animals," Daniel says.

"First we need to rest," I say. "Your head."

"You're right. It's pounding like a team of horses."

Daniel and I move slowly to a perch on a ledge overlooking the water, just far enough away that we can keep on eye on both the boat and the bodies, our silent charges.

"Are you starting to remember?" I ask carefully. "From before?"

"A lot of it is a blur," Daniel says. "Like a streaky photograph or something. You know how it looks if you move while the photographer is taking a picture and the image is a blur of light? My memories are like that. I keep trying to see them, but they're unclear, fuzzy."

The week leading up to Jonathan's death is like that for me. His bed was moved into the front room because it was easier to help him there. The curtains were drawn, the air unmoving. Time seemed to pass so slowly it was as if it wasn't passing at all. There was nothing to mark day from night other than a thin strip of light leaking between the closed drapes. Even now, I can't remember anything specific about those days.

"I remember you told me you're from Parkdale," Daniel offers. "That's right, isn't it? And you have a brother...a twin who died. See? I remember."

I stare at his hands, the veins like blue rope beneath the skin. "What else?"

"Well, I don't remember arguing with my uncle, if that's what you're getting at..."

"I wasn't, actually." I pause. I don't want to start this again. I'm too tired. All my fight is gone. "I'm sorry about that," I say.

He nods. "I'm sorry I called you a liar."

"I wasn't lying. I swear. I did hear you. You were arguing. I was practically standing next to you..."

He raises his eyebrows.

"Sorry."

Daniel leans back on his elbows, knees bent. His hair is finally dry. It's thick and has an unruly curl to it I hadn't noticed before. He glances over at me. "I don't remember arguing on the boat. Really. It's completely gone." He sighs and looks skyward. "But the truth is, my uncle and I have been arguing a lot. Long before we got on the *Asia*. He wants me to do something...something I'm not okay with."

I nod solemnly.

"But it's not what you think. Don't look at me like that. He's not killing people. He's not a murderer. I'm *definitely* not a murderer. I can barely kill a mosquito if it's biting me." Daniel grins before becoming serious again.

"But...my uncle...well, he has no conscience." Daniel winces.

I can't tell if it's pain or his talking about this that hurts, but I don't have a chance to figure it out before he hoists himself to standing.

"My feet are numb. I need to keep moving," he says and starts to walk, setting off along the shore away from the boat and the men. I'm surprised by his energy, but I catch up with him easily.

Daniel stops before stepping across a shallow rock crevice. "Poison ivy," he says, pointing to some green plants with red berries below us. We're up higher here, and I can see the big water out where the boat sank, far past the line of shoals. The lake stretches out endlessly. I'm about to say something, to tell him it's okay if he doesn't want to continue, that we don't have to talk, but he starts up again, as if the words are pouring from him like water from a fountain, unstoppable.

"He raised me—did I mention that? My uncle. My parents couldn't afford to have so many children, so they farmed us out. He used me as slave labor for years. At first it was at a farm his wife's family had passed on to them. I slopped the pigs and mended fences. Slept in the barn. I did everything, really. My aunt was kind. As kind as he'd let her be.

"But when she died in childbirth, he sold her family's land and moved us into town. The land wasn't worth much with all those rocks." Daniel shakes his head. "But it was enough to buy a store. Or enough to look serious. I'm pretty sure he never paid in full. He tricked the widow of the old storekeeper, told her if she gave it to him for cheap, she'd continue to reap profits and not have to do any of the work. I don't think she's seen a penny of the money. She's in love with him too. They always are. He's a charmer. A liar. Taught me everything he knows..." Daniel lets out a small, forced laugh.

I'm afraid to say anything in case he stops talking, stops telling his story. But it also occurs to me, considering his uncle taught him everything he knows, that Daniel could be lying now and I'd never know the difference.

"Where was I?" he asks, looking my way. I'm about to speak, but he starts again. "Oh yeah. My uncle the liar. I'm not sure when I finally realized that everything that came out of his mouth was false. When I was younger I knew he could get people to do anything he wanted. He had that way about him. I admired it. I tried to be like him, as children do. I feared him as well."

I glance behind us and can't see the bodies or the lifeboat anymore. I don't want to get lost or go too far. But Daniel doesn't notice my hesitation. He takes a long step over a stream of water running toward the bay and holds out his hand to help me across. I shake my head to say I'm fine on my own, and he shrugs, keeps talking.

"Later I started to see him for who he truly is," he says. "A trickster, shapeshifter. He roped me into some of his schemes, stuff at the store, giving credit and charging high interest so everyone in town was indebted to him, then making them do stuff that wasn't legal. It was his latest con, though, that I couldn't stand. I just couldn't. At least those people in town knew what they were getting themselves into."

I stumble a bit as we're going down a little slope, and Daniel shoots out a hand to steady me. "Thanks," I say. His hand stays on my upper arm for a second, and I look down at it, confused.

Daniel doesn't seem to notice. "That's probably what we were arguing about," he continues. "On the ship. This latest scheme was the final straw for me. He put advertisements in the newspaper in London. England, you know? Offering investment in a Canadian farm, opportunities for a few good men. Everyone wants to come to Canada, he says. They think there's gold, silver, diamonds under every rock. All those people back on the continent think it's the promised land. There'll be gentlemen, rich gentlemen, who'll want to invest some capital, send their idle, good-for-nothing sons here to look after the investment. We'll be doing them a favor, he says, taking the lazy sods off their hands."

Daniel stops to catch his breath. He sighs deeply. "So he put ads in the *Times of London* and other newspapers. He calls himself a university man—though I'm certain he never spent a minute in school. Says he's looking for a gentleman's son to live with him and learn the ropes of farming with a view to becoming a partner. Asks for five hundred pounds as down payment and promises future profits, opportunities."

Daniel stops walking and rubs his forehead carefully with both hands. He looks pained, his face distorted. "But, of course, there's a catch," he says. "There's always a catch. There's no land worth investing in. He planned to take the money, show the son some patch of swamp and rock, and watch them go crying home to papa." He shrugs. "And guess what? He was right about people being interested. We had two serious responses to the adverts within a month. Rich men with problem sons on their hands, just like he said. I don't feel so sorry for those spoiled prigs, pardon my French, but I don't like cheating people. Plus, he said I had to be involved."

Daniel starts walking again, but he's quiet now. I try to make sense of what he's told me. I've heard about such scams in the newspapers. I remember reading about a swindler using a similar ploy who ended up killing the man he duped, dumping his body in a forest somewhere. He hung for it. I swallow hard, then look away so Daniel can't see my face. Jonathan always said my emotions are written on my eyes, my lips. I can't hide anything.

But Daniel doesn't notice. He's totally absorbed in his story, as if he's hearing it from his own lips for the first time. "My uncle says it's me who has to go over to England to bring the men here, make sure we have the money in the bank before they set foot on Canadian soil. He says I will reassure them with my honest face. I think that's what finally did me in. I'm supposed to be his bait. That's what he called me. *Bait*." Daniel's mouth is set in an angry line. He's picking up his pace now, his strides lengthening.

"We should go back to the lifeboat," I say. "Find something to eat."

Daniel turns to me, looking surprised. "Okay, in a minute," he says. "Just around this corner." He waves vaguely in the direction we're headed, then continues. "I told him I won't do it. I tried to convince him that we'll be caught, that it isn't worth the effort. That it isn't worth the cost of the steamer ticket to send me to England. It sounds deluded, now that I'm saying it out loud, but I think I still hoped he would change. That he actually cared about me..." Daniel *tsks*, shakes his head. "This trip to Toronto, though, it made me realize there's no way that man is ever going to change.

"When I told him I won't do it, that I will go to the police, he tried blackmail," Daniel says. "He said he'll tell the police himself. Said there's nothing linking him to the whole scheme. It's all done in my name. The newspaper advertisement, the bank account."

Daniel lets out a loud sigh and shakes his head. I'm breathing hard now, trying to keep up. Anger is definitely making him come back to life. But he also seems a bit unglued. I look around. The trees loom, their shadows nearly touching our backs.

Daniel stops. "Maybe we *should* go back," he says. He looks down at the rock, where a thick mat of bright green moss is growing around the edge of a shallow puddle. He kicks it, and a piece dislodges, tumbling toward the shoreline.

"I'm in trouble," Daniel says, his voice quieter now. He looks me in the eye. "A lot of trouble maybe. If this gets out, if the police find out, it could be prison for me. There's a lot of money at stake. He's already got the down payment, he told me. So...I guess I'm not surprised you heard us fighting, even if I don't remember it."

The sun is past the midpoint. I almost never pay attention to it at home. Sun warms the roads, makes Mother's kitchen garden grow, but I don't see it, really *see* its daily trajectory tracing the sky above. Today it seems to be crawling, inch by difficult inch. It's almost hot.

"I'm sorry," I say as we begin to walk back.

"For what?" he asks skeptically. "Why are you sorry? It has nothing to do with you. Why do people say that when they have nothing to be sorry for?"

I bristle a bit, then stop myself. "I guess I'm sorry for thinking poorly of you. For suggesting you're a…a thief… when you're clearly…well, you're trying not to be. You're trying to be good."

We track the shoreline back toward the lifeboat. I don't know what else to say. It's a terrible story, yet out here it's like hearing a tale from another land, something you have no way of truly understanding. I think about what Jonathan would do in this situation, and I know he would just listen, let Daniel say what he wants, explain what he needs. Jonathan had a way of letting silence grow and expand and open everyone up to the possibility of something bigger than themselves. That was his secret. He wouldn't talk. Just listen. Then when he did eventually speak, he'd pause for so long between words you could drive a wagon between them. It was as if there was all the time in the world just to finish a sentence. He'd let people find their way through an explanation without filling in the blanks. I'm too impatient. I even finished Jonathan's sentences for him. It drove me crazy how slow he was, though I saw how it made people feel comfortable. They felt heard. I guess I did too.

I hug my arms around my chest, as if this might help me hold my tongue.

"We should make a plan," I say when we finally reach the lifeboat. "Figure out where we're going to sleep tonight. But first you should rest. I can see you wincing. Your head must still be sore."

Daniel doesn't need convincing. He gently removes his coat from the cabin boy and pulls it over his own shoulders. We find a warm patch of rock not too far away. He's asleep within minutes. I stand up, stretch my arms in the air.

I watch the rise and fall of Daniel's shoulders, looping through everything he's just said. All of it makes me wonder about him even more. Is he as reluctant a con man as he claims? Can I truly trust him? Do I have any choice?

It makes me think of my father, who prides himself on being able to read his patients like a book. Most tell him the truth, he says, but there are those with secrets they won't even tell their doctor. Adultery, drink, opium. He says he can tell simply by their mannerisms if they're lying. A twitch of the lip, a toss of the hair, a man rubbing his knuckles. *How much do you drink?* Father will ask, and the alcoholic will invariably look around the empty examining room and say, *Who, me?* as if there are others Father might be asking.

As I'm sitting down, a flash of color in the low-growing bush not far away catches my eye. A sound like leaves crunching under a small foot. There are lots of squirrels and chipmunks in Owen Sound and the Soo. They dart around like their fur's on fire, twitchy, then suddenly calm as they chew on a nut, posing like they're in the funnies.

But there it is again. A flash of movement. Dark, low to the ground.

A snake emerges slowly from the dried-up leaves and juniper bush. It sweeps its body lazily from side to side. I can see markings on its back as it moves onto the rock. Spots or stripes—it's hard to tell from this distance. But it's long. When I think it must be all out of the bush, it just keeps coming. Finally I see its pointy tail, segmented into many rings.

I stop breathing, try to be still. The snake also slows down once it's fully out on the rock. It basks in the heat of the granite, and it looks at least three feet long. I inhale sharply, and the snake turns its head toward me. The markings over its spine are brown and black. Its head is a diamond shape. Rattlesnake.

I rack my brain for everything I've ever heard about rattlesnakes. Before they strike they shake their tails. A warning. The venom is deadly.

My younger cousins used to chop off their heads with shovels every chance they got. There was one that lived under the wide front porch at our grandmother's place in Owen Sound. She wouldn't let the cousins go near it. She said it never hurt her, so why should she hurt it? She said that rattlesnakes are timid unless they're threatened. Once, a barn cat she sometimes fed surprised it and was bitten. It wasn't a pretty death, she said. She told the grandchildren to bang on the stairs to warn it we were coming and we'd never have a problem.

But if they're supposed to be so timid, why is this one headed toward us? It flicks its tiny forked tongue and darts along the rock in my direction.

Ten

Without looking away, I pat my hand over a crack in the rock and find a stone the size of my palm wedged inside. If I wake Daniel suddenly he could provoke the snake by mistake. But I can't just let him lie there and be bitten. I know there are some people who survive a rattlesnake bite, but certainly nobody who is shipwrecked on a rock in the middle of Georgian Bay. There's not a second to waste. I tug the stone out, take a deep breath and throw.

The snake hisses and rears up when the rock lands near its rattle. Its tongue is a blur of motion—forked lightning. Its eyes flash yellow, the pupils tiny slits. It shakes its rattle. I don't know what else to do. I don't dare turn from it. I lock eyes with the snake and scramble with my hand to find another stone. There's just a small one, tiny, really, and I pitch it toward the creature, shouting, *"AAAHHHH!"* like some sort of warrior in battle. What is there to lose?

The snake disappears into the bush before the stone clatters on the rock. I can hear the rustle of leaves as it's swallowed by the forest.

Daniel startles awake and looks at me in confusion. "What's going on?"

I keep my eyes on the bushes where the snake disappeared, my heart ricocheting around my rib cage. There is no sound, just the wind raking through the boughs of the pine and cedar trees behind us. I lean back on the rock and watch the clouds, like fish scales drawn on the sky.

"You missed some excitement," I say.

He raises his eyebrows.

"A snake. A rattler."

"Really?" he asks. "Is it gone?"

"Yep. I scared it off."

"Wow," he says. "You're quite the lady adventurer. Saving me from wild snakes and death by drowning."

I can't tell if he's teasing or thanking me. I look away.

"I didn't mean that in a bad way," he says quickly. "What I meant was, thank you."

"You're welcome," I offer defiantly.

But Daniel's face has softened, and his eyes are wide with exhaustion. "We've had our share of adventures," he says.

"You can say that again." I shrug. And then, for reasons I don't understand myself, I start giggling, and soon I am laughing so hard I can't stop. My stomach aches.

Daniel watches me without speaking.

"I'm sorry," I sputter, trying to get hold of myself. I stand up just to get my breath back. "I'm sorry."

"That's okay. You do that, don't you? Laugh when things are serious."

"Yep, I do. It's my curse. How's your head, anyway?"

"Better," Daniel says. "There's still a dull roar, but it's duller, better." He looks down at the rock, then out at the water. He pauses as if he wants to say something more but stops himself.

"Maybe we should try to move along the shore in the boat, see if there's anything else nearby," I say. "Something to eat. Berries. I'm starving."

"Yeah, me too." Daniel sighs deeply and clears his throat. "I just need to ask you something. You know all that stuff I told you? Well...I shouldn't have said anything. I shouldn't have told you about my uncle. If he's alive, he'll be furious. Promise me you'll forget about it. This is serious. Please?"

I offer Daniel a hand to help him to his feet. He accepts it, and I lean my whole body back to counterbalance his weight. "Okay," I say when we're standing, though I think we both know better than to believe I'll forget. Not his story, not these days and hours adrift. Nothing.

Daniel drops my hand and pats down his clothes self-consciously. He avoids looking me in the eye. "We still need to bury them," he says. "Or at least cover them up. Mark the shore with some branches. That way we know where they are. We can come back if we know the spot is marked."

It's a good idea, though the thought of going near the dead men again makes my heart sink. Daniel suggests I look for branches, leaves and bark on the edge of the tree line. I nod but don't move while he heads off in the opposite direction. I take a few half-hearted steps.

"Maybe we could stay together?" I call, and he nods, waves his hand for me to join him.

It takes a long time to find enough leaves, branches, needles and sticks to cover the five bodies. We move painstakingly back and forth from the trees to the men, resting often, as if we are making offerings in a slow, solemn ceremony. When we're done, we haul smallish stones from the shore to mark the perimeter. Daniel wedges a thick branch upright between some larger rocks as a kind of crude marker that can be seen from the water. The sun is beginning to move lower in the sky. We take a long break to rest, drink water and plot our next move.

"We should say a few words," Daniel says, his hands cupped, water dripping from his chin. "For the men."

The two of us stand side by side at the head of the makeshift grave, looking out toward the water. We've done a pretty good job, all things considered. A crazy quilt of brown and red pine needles, green branches and sticks, the largest on top so the whole thing doesn't blow away.

Without agreeing to do so, we both begin to whisper the Lord's Prayer.

Deliver us from evil. The words ring in my head after we say them. Is what's happened to us evil? Punishment for some transgression, some cruelty? The devil's work? Or is it all just bad luck? A terrible storm, an overloaded boat, bad judgment, bad timing. Was the rattlesnake evil or just being a snake, and we happened to land on its rock? Surely it's self-centered, self-absorbed, to consider ourselves touched by some specific, us-sized evil rather than simply victims of circumstance.

Frankly, I think I'd rather be subject to circumstance—as devastating as it is—because it is also knowable, something I can break down into its component parts. Evil, it seems to me as I stand with the bodies of five innocent dead men at our feet, is the creation of people who can't or won't accept that bad things happen. They just happen. And they happen to good people. All the time.

And somehow, here on this rock, facing the lake, warm sun on my face, this doesn't make me feel despair or anger or confusion. I know it's not a good thing or a bad thing. It's not something I need to embrace or to fight. It doesn't make me feel abandoned or solitary. In fact, standing here, whispering into the wind and water, blue lake and sky meeting in a line at the edge of the earth, speaking for the souls of these dead men, I feel more alive, more purposeful, than I have since my twin brother died.

When we finish our prayer, Daniel and I stand still. The wind has picked up, pushing my hair from my face. I say a private farewell to my cousin, and to the captain and cabin boy, to Mr. Sullivan and Mr. McAllister too. And I know with a certainty that rises up from the water, the rock and the lichen, through my boots and into my body, that everything has changed. There will be no more running away. Not now. Not ever. I'm not going to find Jonathan, and running won't help me find myself. I have to face my fate, face life. But this time it's not dramatic or silly. It's the real thing.

When I feel Daniel's hand reaching for mine, I take it gladly. He squeezes my fingers like a promise. His hand is bigger than mine, cool and dry. We stand silently, arm to arm, hands locked together as the wind rustles the leaves and gently shifts some of the smaller branches over the grave.

"It's getting late," he says eventually. "We should go down the shore like you said. Look for food. See if there's anything. Anything else."

I squeeze back.

It takes less effort than I expected to get the boat off the rock. A big shove. A sigh. We stay as close to the shore-line as possible without running aground. Daniel uses the oar to push off the bottom, and I do the same with a strong, thick branch I found. It's exhausting work, and we have to stop often. I'm so hungry now that my head feels spinny. My thoughts bounce around like soap bubbles, forming and then popping or floating away.

Daniel grimaces and grunts with each pry. I don't think he even knows he's doing it. We push and pole ourselves around a tip of land that juts out into the water. I glance back over my shoulder, thinking it might be the last we'll see of the men we buried. I spot the thick branch still standing upright, marking the place.

The lifeboat is light now without the men, but it's still not easy to maneuver. We stay in the shallows near shore, but there's much banging on the rock and having to get out to push off. I lean over and see greeny-yellow rocks just under the surface. When we move they disappear, darkness opening like a hole below. It's hard to calculate the depth or danger.

After a half hour I barely have enough energy to put the branch in the water. We agree to coast for a minute in a narrow channel sheltered from the wind.

"It's an island," Daniel says as we catch our breath. "Where we landed."

I don't know how he knows this, but I'm too tired to ask.

"I've been watching. See that little channel? It divides this island from the one we landed on."

I look around. I'm not sure how he can distinguish any part of this shore from another. It all looks the same to me. Smoother near the big water, craggy boulders, rock and tangled brush closer to us, taller trees beyond. It's a relentless green-and-brown scribble.

We start up again. I'm dizzy, light-headed with hunger and lack of sleep. I don't know if we're going anywhere at all.

"There's an inside channel around somewhere," Daniel calls. "I'll know it when I see it. It's the way people go from village to village by water. Steamers too. It's deep."

I don't say anything. Every once in a while Daniel calls from the bow—"Hard right!" or "Push left!"—and I try my best to do as he says. But I start drifting, thinking about my friend Ally and how I didn't say goodbye. She didn't deserve that. She tried so hard to help me through Jonathan's illness and death, and I pushed her away again and again. I try to picture her sweet, heart-shaped face. She has such a gentle look that people are surprised by her sharp tongue.

When the metal hull bangs hard against a rock, I nearly skewer myself with the branch as I fall forward. Water splashes up and soaks me. "Watch it!" I shout.

"You okay?" he asks.

I rub my hip. It's tender. "You might have warned me!"

"Sorry," he says.

I wipe my face with the already wet sleeve of my dress and watch him return to pushing off. It's not his fault we hit the shore or that I fell over. Still, I don't apologize. I return to poling off the rock with my branch, trying to focus on the task, though my arms are tired and my fingers frozen.

We don't speak for a long time. I can hear his labored breathing, and I disappear back into my remembering.

We finally rest again in another channel. There seems to be a gentle current here. Wispy whirlpools dance in the water, erratic and determined. I spot a low rock face on the shore that looks as if it has been cleaved off from the land. It's flat, facing the channel, and its top end is squared off. There's a crack like a mouth near the bottom.

"A whale," I say out loud.

"Pardon?" Daniel asks, still breathing heavily.

"The rock. It's shaped like a whale. See the big head?"

Daniel doesn't respond. He must think I'm completely addled now. Laughing hysterically about things that aren't funny, yelling at him, pointing out shapes in the rock. But then he speaks. "I see it. Moby Dick."

I shoot him a grin that I hope he understands is part gratitude, part apology. And maybe he does understand, because he starts reciting again, his hands forming words in the air.

"And now there came both mist and snow,
And it grew wondrous cold:
And ice, mast-high, came floating by,
As green as em-er-ald."

"'Rime of the Ancient Mariner'?" I ask.

"You know it?"

"Not really. But I saw a copy in your pocket when you were out cold. After you hit your head."

Daniel pats his jacket and screws up his eyebrows.

"I needed a hanky to soak up the blood. The book was in your pocket."

"Oh," he says. "I can't get that stanza out of my mind. I keep wondering, is the water here *as green as em-er-ald?*"

"Yeah," I say, as if this is a perfectly obvious thing to wonder under the circumstances. We each return to silent contemplation. We finally pull the boat up behind a crooked point guarding a shallow bay that ends in reeds. We're in the shadows here, the sun behind the trees, and it's cooler, a promise of what will come when it gets dark. Trying to step out of the boat, I nearly fall flat on my back once again. I'm boneless, dizzy. I can only imagine how useless I'll be after another night without food, without shelter.

"Over there," Daniel says when we're sitting down. He extends a finger toward a spit of land in the distance. "We should head there."

I can see a bare, high rock facing the bay. But to get there we'll have to cross windy, open water strewn with shoals, some with water breaking over them, others poking up just above the waves. There's no way we can do it if Daniel is even half as tired as I am.

"Maybe we should stay here," I offer. "Spend the night. It's sheltered. It might be warmer out of the wind. And there's a marsh. There could be something we could eat. I've heard you can eat bulrushes. The roots. The stalk too. Raw...I think."

Daniel looks at me with eyebrows raised.

"My granny told me," I protest. "She knew about stuff like that."

"Well, maybe so...though I've never heard that. But I saw something over there. I didn't want to say until we were closer. I'm sure it's not a tree. I think it's...I think it's man-made."

I squint, tracking the line where land meets the sky, but can't see anything out of the ordinary. Still, remembering how angry and withdrawn he became when I didn't see the light earlier, I swallow my misgivings. The truth is, I'm too weak to care where we go. If we don't find food, we're doomed anyway. "Okay," I say.

Daniel helps me into the lifeboat and pushes us from shore with a new sense of urgency. He sweeps the oar in the water one way, then the other. But the wind quickly blows us off course. I watch through heavy lids, helpless with my branch in the deeper water. The shore we're headed for remains blurry, the water a shimmering mass. I can't make out detail, just color and light, but I see we're far off where Daniel wanted to go.

About halfway across the channel Daniel takes a rest, and the boat drifts. There are shoals everywhere.

"What are you doing?" I call, panic in my voice. He doesn't remember what happened when we ran aground earlier, but I do.

"I just need a break...I can't...I can't..." He lets the oar clatter to the floor of the lifeboat.

Danger sharpens my thinking. I move quickly to the bow, trying not to rock the boat, and take the oar from him, urging Daniel to go back toward the stern. My mind is clear for the first time in hours. I lean over and sweep the oar through the water.

"You see the thing I was telling you about?" he calls.

"Yeah, I think so. It's starting to come into focus," I lie. "Over there?" I wave one hand toward the shore.

"Yes! That's it! That's it!"

I can't bear to look at him. He's hallucinating again. *"As green as em-er-ald…"*

I try to think only about my breathing, in and out, counting to four with each inhale and exhale. I'm not thinking, just doing. And the crazy thing is, we're making headway. Maybe the wind came up behind us, or we hit a new current that straightened our course. But when the boat hits the high, rocky shore, I barely have time to brace myself. I grip the sides of the lifeboat, and our only oar is pitched into the water.

Eleven

The hull is wedged sideways. It bangs hard on the low cliff, waves from the open water smashing us again and again against the rock. It's not a very steep face, but it's too high and craggy, the waves too strong for us to get out of the boat safely. If the wind comes up, we'll be bashed to smithereens.

Daniel's eyes burn like a fever. "Let's go! Let's go!" he calls.

I look around, panicking, uncertain what he wants me to do. There's flash of wood in the water, and the oar bobs up. It's trapped between the shore and the boat.

I don't think we can retrieve it without crushing our hands, but Daniel doesn't hesitate. He points to the branch, urging me to use it to hold the boat away from the rock while he leans in to fish out the oar. It takes a few attempts, but he finally pulls it back on board, his knuckles and arm bloodied from the rocky cliff.

We propel ourselves quickly along the face using our hands and the branch, moving toward a low point where we can tie up and get out. The trees closest to the water here are skeletal, twisted by the wind, leaning away from the open bay as if frightened by its force. The forest behind is dense, a solid mass of green.

As soon as we finish tying up, Daniel is gone, off to search for whatever he thought he saw from the other shore. His exhaustion forgotten, he is possessed suddenly by some otherworldly energy, and I trail behind, up and down, dodging prickly juniper and barren raspberry bushes.

I can no longer see him when he calls out, "That's it! That's it!"

The slope is steep, and I can't see what he's talking about. I use both hands and feet to clamber up, my wet boots nearly useless on the rock. When I make it to the highest point, I find Daniel bouncing around like a child at Christmas. There's a large barrel beside him, propped up on top of a thick branch wedged into a cut in the rock. It's the kind of barrel a shop might use to transport flour or apples or whiskey.

After all this time adrift, I find it jarring somehow to see something made by a human hand. It looks, in fact, as if the barrel has been placed here intentionally.

"I told you!" he says. "I knew it! I've heard about this place. Fishermen and sailors call it Pointe au Baril!"

"Someone will find us," he adds. "I know it now."

I look around. It's the same trees, same rock, as all along this forbidding coast. The view out to the open water is vast, blue as far as I can see. I want to believe Daniel, but rescue seems as unlikely to me now as it ever did.

"Come. Look," he says, kneeling down beside the barrel. A portion of the wooden side has been cut out. "Smell it," he says.

I lean in and catch the unmistakable scent of kerosene. I cough.

"I wasn't sure if it existed at all outside the talk of sailors on the Manitowaning docks," he says. "But here it is. True as my heart." He's nearly breathless, and I'm surprised again to feel a tenderness for this boy and his ability to rally over and over despite everything. It's a feeling that starts in my throat and radiates outward, filling my hands and feet with pins and needles.

"The story I heard was that an old fur-trade canoe was wrecked years ago, a barrel of whiskey lost." He slaps the wood with his open hand. "The next spring some traders found it and drank it dry. They left the barrel here as a marker. People put kerosene lanterns inside. Helps guide them along the shore. It's been here for decades."

Daniel inspects the barrel again while I sit on the rock, thinking about how the two of us seem to take turns swinging wildly between elation and terror, despair and hope. I don't really know what to think about his theory, but hope, even vain hope, is surely better than fear.

My stomach rumbles, and I manage to convince Daniel that even if we're going to be rescued, we should probably look around for something to eat. We walk back and retie the lifeboat, moving it along to a sheltered bay. We place the oar on the shore, far from the water's edge. But when we're finished we're both too tired to search for food or anything else. We find a smooth rock and sit down, and both of us fall asleep immediately.

❖　　❖　　❖

The sun is sinking lower in the sky when I wake up. Daniel is beside me, lying on his side. His legs are tucked up to his belly, his eyeballs racing beneath flickering eyelids. My mind is fuzzy again. There's a hole in my stomach as deep as a well.

We're definitely going to have to spend another night out here. Another night without shelter or food. Another night knowing we may not make it to morning. I touch Daniel's arm and jostle him gently.

"Huh?" he asks, opening one eye, then the other. He looks like someone still in a dream, one arm thrown over his face. His hair is messy, his coat loose, shirt collar gaping like an open door. Despite our circumstances, despite the cold and desolation, something about the way he's flung his arm, his crumpled clothing, reminds me of those mornings in early winter when it's dark outside and you don't want to get out of bed. You only want to sink down farther into your covers, forever tossed between sleep and wakefulness. Even as I am conjuring this peaceful feeling, I wonder if I will ever feel that way again.

"I'm afraid," I say. "I'm afraid we're going to die. Today. Tonight. Right here."

Daniel sits up, leans back against his elbows. "Don't you see?" he says, his tone kind but insistent. "The barrel means that people pass by here. All the time." His face softens more. "I told you, I've heard about it. Fishermen, lumbermen, trappers—they come by. It's part of the navigation channel. Someone is going to find us. And if they don't, well, at least we know where we are. We know now where we have to go."

I shake my head, eyes cast down. My tangled hair falls in front of my face. I don't even notice Daniel has reached for me until I feel the tips of his fingers on my chin, tilting my face toward him so I have to look him in the eye. He parts the curtain of my hair with his other hand.

"It's going to be all right. I promise." He grins, then drops his hand to the rock.

It all happens so quickly, I might have imagined his hands on my face, his fingers in my hair. I want to say something, but my mouth is dry. It won't obey my brain. It feels as if my lips are contorted into an unnatural smile. I force my mouth closed, press my lips together.

I want to believe him. But more than that, I want him to touch me again. I want him to hold me and tell me again that everything is going to be okay, even if it's not. Instead, I sit up and move away.

"Sorry," he says.

"No," I sputter. "I just...I just need to get up. Maybe we should find some leaves or something to keep us warm overnight, a spot beneath the trees to sleep. It's going to be getting dark soon."

I shiver so much my teeth begin to chatter. What am I thinking? Leaves aren't going to keep us warm. We need food, proper shelter. We'll be discovered in the spring, frozen solid beneath the boughs. But before I can take back my words, Daniel stands up beside me.

"You're cold," he says.

"Uh-hmm." I nod. Yes. Yes. But mostly I'm scared. Scared by how much I long for his touch and how little I know how to ask for it.

But Daniel is already taking a small step toward me. He puts his arms around the tops of my shoulders, awkwardly trapping my arms by my side like a straitjacket. I'm afraid to move, to shift, in case he takes it as a sign I don't want this. I do. When Daniel pulls his coat around us, I have a chance to adjust my arms, wrapping them around him. We hold each other, and a warmth that has nothing to do with the coat floods through me, making my cheeks burn.

"We're going to be all right. We're going to make it. I promise," he whispers. I can feel his breath on the top of my head, and it makes me feel tense and reckless at the same time.

"Don't," I say quietly. "Don't promise."

"I promise," he says more definitively.

I turn my face so that my cheek is resting on his chest just below his chin. He turns his head too. We both look out at the water. It's calm now, a mirror of the darkening sky. My heart, though, seems to be auditioning for a position in a brass marching band. I'm hugging him so hard that when I release slightly, I can hear his breath catch in his throat. We stay that way for a long time. Everywhere he holds me, I feel safe.

Just when I'm beginning to think neither of us will speak, that we will stay this way forever, he says, "I know what I said before, but I'm glad I told you about my uncle." He pulls his head back so he can see my face, keeping his arms around my back. "I've never told anyone before. It actually feels good, to be honest."

Daniel swallows hard. I can see his Adam's apple moving up and down. "It's hard for me to trust people, I guess.

But I've been thinking...if he's gone, maybe now I have a chance. Maybe I can start again. I can stop pretending all the time that things are okay. I'm not like you. You don't seem to ever pretend. You say exactly what you think."

I shake my head, but I can't speak. Words are trapped in my throat.

"But I'm not okay. And I haven't been for a long time," Daniel says. "I wanted my life to be what people thought it was, for my uncle to be the man other people thought he was. And even though...even though it's terrible, well...I hope he's dead." He swallows again, releases me a little, but I hug him just a bit more tightly.

"It sounds awful...but it's true. After everything...after everything that's happened, I feel I can say it to you. I can trust you. Maybe you're the only person I *can* trust."

I look up at him, and he's looking down at me, and I'm about to say, *You can—you can trust me*, but before the words are out of my mouth, he's pressing his lips against mine. There's a tingling around my ears shooting downward through my body, and I kiss him back. The world outside us disappears. We're underwater. Out of air, out of time. His lips are soft but not yielding. They push against mine like a challenge, and I open my mouth just a little, press my tongue against his lips, pry them open slightly.

He makes a noise like he's hurt. I think he's going to pull away, but instead he pushes his tongue back. I'm not sure where I stop and he begins.

But then Daniel drops his arms from around my back and takes my face in his hands, cupping my cheeks at my jawline, pulling away to look at me. He smiles.

I offer him an uncertain grin in return. My lips feel swollen, as if they have been stung. He leans over and kisses me again. This time it's over in a second.

"All right," he says, pulling away. "We better find a spot to spend the night before it's dark. The sun is nearly gone."

I stand still for a second, my body humming. Daniel steps away, then looks back at me.

"I do pretend!" I say. "I pretend all the time!"

Daniel raises his eyebrows.

"Like when I told you I was going to visit my aunt in the Soo," I blurt out. "I'm not visiting anyone. I ran away from home. I had to go. No one except you even knows I was on the *Asia*. Well, Peter, but he's..."

I swipe my hand across my mouth like I've just slurped up water. My skin is hot to the touch.

Daniel reaches his hand out. "Come on," he says, motioning for me to join him.

We find a tall pine with low-hanging branches that are just high enough we can sit up straight underneath them. The reddish brown needles are surprisingly soft. Daniel passes me a short, thick branch, and we begin to dig into the soil. We carve a nest from the ground, then layer it with more pine needles and whatever other soft material we can find— some green boughs and a few leaves. We look for food, too, but there's nothing we recognize.

The two of us work quickly, searching for soft materials, digging, moving in unison. Piling up the debris, my hand brushes against his, and I feel that same flush I did earlier. It spreads through my body like the underground forest fires I've read about. There are no flames on the ground, and everyone thinks the fire has been put out, but it's only gone beneath the soil, lighting up the roots and dead vegetation. It smolders, sometimes burning slowly all winter long, only to emerge at the surface in springtime, undaunted, stronger than ever.

I want to say something, want to acknowledge whatever it is that's happening between us, but I'm too tired and uncertain. Perhaps there are no words. Maybe this is one of those times when trying to find language that fits only ruins things. We smile at each other when we're finished, pleased with our handiwork.

It's nearly dark by the time we burrow deep into the pine needles and soft boughs. Lying close together, we watch the stars pop out of the sky, the Milky Way smeared like sparkling paint across the surface. He takes my hand and squeezes gently. Every part of me that is not touching him is extra, unnecessary. I want to kiss him again, and I want him to kiss me, but I can hardly move. My head is spinning, and my legs and arms feel like they are sinking into the rock beneath us, merging with the ground.

I must drift off, because I'm startled when Daniel whispers loudly, "Did you hear that?"

I don't hear anything. I can't even see Daniel it's so dark. But as my eyes begin to adjust, I can make out shapes, the place where the forest ends and rock takes over, the water just beyond. A partial moon glowing behind the clouds.

The trees crack and groan in the wind. I start to speak, to reassure Daniel, but then I do hear something. Something moving through the undergrowth, bushes parting. It sounds bigger than a snake. Bigger than a red squirrel.

Bigger, perhaps, than us. The ground beneath us rumbles. It's coming closer.

Daniel's fingers tighten over mine. He sits up. He places a single finger on my lips, pressing with purpose. A gamy animal smell drifts toward us on the wind—musky, like wet wool and sweat. If we can smell it, it can surely smell us.

We can hear the creature breathing. It's loud. Close. We don't move for a long time, and the sounds stop too. We are frozen in a standoff. But then Daniel lets out a tiny, nearly inaudible gasp, as if he was holding his breath and couldn't do it anymore, and the creature bolts, crashing through the bushes away from us.

Daniel's face is pale and angular in the light of the moon. *Bear*, he mouths, eyes wide.

"You think it's still here?" I whisper.

He grips my hand again. We listen to the forest and hear only the creak of swaying trees, crickets, frog song. Water laps softly against the shore. I'm so hungry now my stomach is no longer even making noise. I'm shutting down. I start to drift off again.

I don't know how long I've been asleep—minutes? hours?—before Daniel shakes my arm again, and I bolt upright. Branches are crashing. The ground is moving. It's louder than before. I have felt near death so many times over the last days. I have straddled the line between hope and despair, exhilaration and helplessness. But right now we aren't helpless. We can do something. We *have* to do something.

"Come on!" I whisper to Daniel and tug his hand. He pulls back, hesitating. But as I rise to my feet, he stands beside me.

I start shouting, "Go away! Go away!" I wave my arms and can see Daniel is doing the same thing.

We shout, "Aarrragh!" Jump up and down, kick the ground, stomp.

And in the light of the moon I can see the creatures, half in, half out of the bush nearest us. There are two of them, standing still as stone, faces poking from the bushes. They have wet brown noses and pointy, oversized ears. Their eyes are like saucers. Deer.

We keep yelling and stomping for a few seconds more before the animals thunder off into the bush. Then, with our voices still echoing in the stillness, we look at each other. I start laughing first. It's the kind of laughter that's full of relief, tinged with hysteria. And he starts laughing too. The sound fills the sky like starlight. It's hard to stop, and I have to lean over, brace my hand against my knee and breathe deeply. My corset digs into the top of my leg, and when I adjust it I feel the outline of my cousin's logbook. The memory of his children's faces is sharp. It slices through this moment like a scythe. I remember everything.

"Come on," Daniel says, settling back into our improvised bed. He pats the ground beside him, and I lie down, pulling my hair up around my head. It's surprisingly warm and comfortable here in the shadow of the pine tree.

I remember everything, but I don't feel afraid anymore. Not of bears or snakes or deer or shipwrecks or this strange buzzing feeling in my body as if I'm a city alight with electricity for the first time. I feel as if I could paddle us all the way to Parry Sound on my own. Yes, I'm hungry and dizzy, but I'm alive. I'm alive.

"Daniel?" I say, moving onto my side.

"Uh-huh?" he says, turning his head toward me.

I move in closer. He's breathing loudly, and I arch my back to tuck into his body. Our noses mash, and we both smile a little. I lean in farther. Our lips meet again. I'm alive.

Twelve

The water is so cold it burns my throat. But I have to drink. My mouth feels like I've been eating dirt—it's gritty and thick. I'm stiff, my back aches, and my limbs are like heavy logs.

I woke up tucked under Daniel's arm. He was so still that I thought at first he was dead. I checked his chest in a panicky daze. But his breathing was steady.

I untangled myself, trying not to disturb him, and sat still in the shadow of the forest, watching him inhale and exhale, his face calm, skin pale. Was last night a dream? Did he hold me? Kiss me? Did I kiss him? Was it just inquisitive deer, or was there a bear out there in the bush too? Are our fears outsized or exactly right? Is today the day we will die?

I watch the light emerge from the horizon. It is completely still this morning, not a ripple on the water, not even a gentle wave lapping the shore. I can see a few minnows darting among the fuzzy stones covered in green algae. The darkened rock is slippery, and I use one hand to hold myself steady as

I crouch, glancing up and down the shore. I see the barrel at the highest spot on the point. Daniel's great hope.

I don't want to be a killjoy, but we have to be realistic. We can't sit here and wait for someone to come. We have to leave this barren rock. Today. Soon. And we have to find something to eat or we are definitely not going to make it anywhere.

I'm rising, bracing my back with one hand, when I hear the *hwah* of a seagull. It's floating overhead, wings outstretched, and I remember the bird that landed on the lifeboat. Was that only yesterday? The seagull flies away and then back toward me, searching for something in the water. I search, too, but see nothing.

It feels as if the solid rock beneath my boots is spinning. I close my eyes, and when I open them I *do* spot something in the water. It's out by the point, drifting slowly, partly submerged. It's long and dark.

I swallow the ache in my throat. "Daniel?" I call, fear unmistakable in my voice. "Daniel?" He's up and by my side in seconds. "A body," I say. "I think there's a body."

I don't let my eyes leave the object. Daniel searches the water where I'm pointing, then launches himself up the rock toward the barrel, where there's a better view. Up high, we can see there are actually many things in the water. And in a little cove on the other side of the point, something white is draped over a large rock.

The other object has moved closer to the same cove. If we want to retrieve it, we'll have to negotiate a steep slope. Daniel goes ahead, and I follow in my slippery boots. He gets to the white thing first. It's heavy and dripping wet. He turns it over in his hands, water pouring onto his feet. A pillowcase.

We both see the name *Asia* stitched along the hem at the same time. He drops it on the rock. The pillowcase smacks the stone, sticks where it lands.

There is something about this evidence of the wreck that makes everything seem suddenly more terrible and more real. Since we buried the others, I have been caught in a strange and foggy reverie. But now...Now there's no escaping what happened to us or to the others on the ship.

Not far from where we're standing I see something else on the shore. It looks like a life preserver, the cottony kapok insides hanging out of a tear in the fabric like stuffing from an old doll. The object I thought was a body is nearly close enough to reach. It's bigger than it looked, and there's a flicker of something red.

"Paint," I say, my voice quiet.

"It's part of a boat," Daniel says.

It's definitely wood, slightly curved. Maybe part of the hull of a dinghy or that canoe I saw on the *Asia*'s deck. It thumps against the shore, breaking into splinters as the seagull floats overhead, circling back to watch us. The wood is useless. There's no point trying to retrieve it. We make our way up and over the high point back to our own boat.

It's going to be another bright, cool fall day. The wind is picking up. I can see little whitecaps building on the open water. Another time, I might feel soothed by this breeze, by the morning light with its warm honey glow. But the wreckage casts a pall over everything. If last night's kiss made me imagine some other story about all this, some other less horrible ending, it's obvious now that I was deluded. The only thing that matters in this moment, on this rock, is survival.

We are survivors. If we make it to the mainland, it will be up to us to speak for those who didn't. It will be up to us to tell their stories. The responsibility is heavy on my shoulders.

We're nearly at the lifeboat when Daniel reaches out a hand to help me get down a short slope. His fingers are warm, his hand enclosing mine. But I quickly pull away. We can't afford to dwell in this fiction any longer.

I've been fooling myself thinking that all of this has changed me. I'm the same selfish girl Mother always said I am. Even last night I was thinking only about myself when there is so much more at stake.

We sit down on the rock, looking south over the channel we crossed yesterday, watching the rhythmic movement of the small waves. I steel myself. I have to stop this. Daniel needs to know who I am. What kind of impatience, what kind of cruelty, I'm capable of.

"This isn't the first time I've run away," I tell him as we watch the water. "The first time was right after my brother died. I didn't think about anyone else. I just left. I wasn't even sad. Not at first."

Daniel nods kindly.

"No. You don't understand. I just left. I didn't say a word. I didn't tell anyone where I was going. I wandered out of Parkdale into one of the ravines in Toronto. I stumbled around down there in the muck and mud and garbage. I was like a lunatic. Then the creek began to shrink and the slope of the riverbank flattened out until I emerged at the street that cuts across the top of Toronto. Bloor. It's more like a country road, really. My boots were filthy, the hem of my dress torn and covered in dirt. When I saw a woman hustle her daughter to the other side of the street, I put my hand to my head and realized how ridiculous I must have looked without a hat, my hair tangled and loose." I laugh glumly. "Look at me now..."

Daniel shrugs but doesn't speak.

"Even then I didn't care. What was shame compared to the fact that my brother was gone?"

Daniel puts his hand on my shoulder, but I shift away. "No. Don't. Listen to me. I followed Bloor Street as buildings gave way to little garden plots and then farmers' fields. Sometimes I'd hear the clip-clop of hooves and the clucking of a wagon driver, and I'd shuffle off to the side. I finally stopped where another river rose up from the south. The edge of High Park. I turned into the woods and began to head for the willow trees that line the pond. I was looking for my brother. My dead brother."

Daniel picks up my hand and presses his lips gently to my palm. He smiles at me, and I think I'm going to cry for gratitude, for the pleasure of his touch. But I shake my head and pull my hand away.

"I ran away. Don't you see? I didn't think about my parents or my best friend Ally, who must have been worried sick. My twin brother had just died, and I took off. Jonathan would have comforted everyone if it were me instead of him. But I didn't think how they would feel or how it would look to others. I didn't think about how people would see me as a streetwalker or a maniac. I thought only of myself." I look at Daniel again, expecting my words to provoke him, but he just nods for me to continue.

"I stayed away all night. I lay on my back, just like last night, watching the black sky, stars blinking in the vastness.

I didn't even know why I was there. Not at first. Maybe not even until right now. But I think maybe the picnic we had there with all of our friends is one of my last happy memories before Jonathan's illness confused everything. I was like those homing pigeons I've read about that the French used during the siege of Paris to send messages in and out of the city. They just knew where they had to go. It was an instinct, a need so deep inside it was impossible not to heed, equally impossible to explain. I couldn't explain. Not to my parents. Or Ally. Not even to myself."

I hesitate, but Daniel encourages me to continue. "I woke up in the morning covered in dew, and, just like today, my limbs were locked, my fingers so stiff I could hardly flex them. But the thing I remember is that my mind was strangely, indescribably free. I remembered Jonathan, and I cried for him. I cried for the cool morning that he would never feel again. I cried for the blossoms in the trees that he would never smell, the grass that would never again tickle his neck, the poems he would never write. And I cried for myself."

"I'm sorry," Daniel says, inching closer to me.

"But the stupid thing is, the really stupid thing, is I thought that was it. I thought I'd grieved. I'd done my mourning. But it turns out I just have to keep doing it over and over and over again."

I haven't cried since that day in the park. Not at Jonathan's funeral. Not when we buried him. Not when we buried my cousin and the other men just yesterday. But I can feel the tears building up now against the back of my throat.

Daniel moves close enough that he can put his arm around my shoulders and pull me toward him. This time I don't push him away. I can't. The trees behind us groan. Water piles up against the shore. I press my cheek to Daniel's chest and give in to wave upon wave of tears so violent and unstoppable that my body shudders and heaves. All the time, Daniel never stops holding me. He must be exhausted himself, but he keeps rubbing my arm, patting my hair, and for the first time since Jonathan died, I don't run away. I allow myself to be comforted.

When I finally stop crying, I turn my back to Daniel and wipe my eyes and nose with my sleeve. I don't want to show him my deranged crying face, blotchy and red.

"It's okay," he says, gently turning me around by my shoulders. He lifts my chin like he did that first time he touched me, and I have to look at him. "Christina, listen to me. Stop beating yourself up. You're not your brother. And you're not awful or cruel. You were just trying to deal with losing him. Even running away doesn't seem strange to me. You lost part of yourself. No one else can understand how that feels. And anyway, we can't always do what other people want us to do. Sometimes we have to choose our own way, even if it's not the easy one. Especially if it's not."

His face is serious. I search it for cracks, a flicker of doubt, reproach. But there is nothing. He doesn't let go of my chin.

Finally, he drops his hand to the rock and picks up a pebble, holding it in his palm as if weighing it. I watch him, letting his words soak in, trying to believe him.

"How did a shop boy get to be so smart?" I tease.

Daniel holds up his hands, palms in the air, and shrugs. We both smile.

"But if I'm so smart," he says, his voice dropping a register, "why hasn't anyone come by yet? I was so sure. I thought we were as good as rescued when we saw the barrel."

I lean into him and reach for his hand. I weave my fingers through his and squeeze.

"It's going to be all right," I say. "I promise."

I move closer and press my lips against his neck. He shivers. All the noise of the wind is drowned out. I can only hear the roar of our breath, his heart. He pulls me toward him, one hand at my waist.

I rest my head on his shoulder and burrow my face into his neck. He smells warm, musky.

"Christina?" he says.

"Uh-hmmm," I say.

"Christina!"

"Yeah?" I lift my cheek from his shoulder.

"No, I mean *look!* Christina, *look!*" He pushes me away slightly.

I feel a stab of regret. I've put myself out—kissed him, held him. Things I would never do, wouldn't think of doing, if we weren't out here in the wilderness, if death didn't seem so close, if he hadn't done it first. If he wants to show me another piece of wreckage, I'm not going to be able to muster the energy to respond. I just can't.

"There!" he says, pointing past the barrel.

It looks like big whitecaps. The waves are getting much larger. "Yeah. The wind is coming up." I try not to allow disappointment into my voice.

"No! A sail! Don't you see it? There's a sail. I'm sure of it."

I squint into the wind. On the horizon, far in the distance, I see something white—bigger than a whitecap, smaller than a ship. Maybe it's a sail, but it could be something else. It's too far away to tell what it is or even if it's headed in our direction.

But Daniel jumps to his feet. "We have to find a way to attract their attention. We have to get them to see us." He looks around frantically. I stand up and do the same. I'm not sure that moving quickly is going to change anything, but I suppose it can't hurt.

There's nothing—no fire to send up smoke signals, no flags to wave. There's the oar back by the boat, Daniel's coat, some branches maybe. We can get some really big ones in the woods near where we slept.

"The pillowcase!" I shout and run back up and over the high point toward the cove. I slip on the wet rock and slide down on my backside. I'm winded and bruised, my vision blurry as I rise to standing, but there's no time for worry. I pick up the pillowcase, fold it over and wring out the water, then wring it again. I wrap it over on itself and squeeze one more time.

Daniel is half carrying, half dragging the oar toward the top of the slope when I return. I help him get it the final few feet to the high rock near the barrel. I'm weak and dizzy again, my arms and legs sore. I have to place each foot carefully or I'm going to fall.

We pull the pillowcase over the oar and hoist it in the air. Daniel waves it back and forth a few times. But the whole thing is too heavy for him to do on his own. We wedge one end in a small slit in the rock and stand on either side, moving the oar together like we're stirring a pot with a giant wooden spoon. The pillowcase is still too wet to move much in the wind, but it might catch someone's eye if we're lucky.

Daniel starts to shout. "Here! We're here! Heeeelp! We need heeeelp!"

Whoever or whatever it is, is too far away to hear anything with the wind blowing toward us, but I join in anyway. "Heeeellllp!"

We have to rest after a few minutes. "I'm so dizzy," I say. "I need to sit down. Just for a minute."

Daniel nods. I see a stick on the ground and pick it up to inspect it. It's thick and short, about the length of my forearm. I scrape it idly against the rock. My father always told us an empty barrel makes the most noise—a reminder to hold our tongues unless we had something worthwhile to say. I test out his theory with a tap against the barrel, and it makes such a dull thud, the sound won't carry at all. I bang the stick against the wood in different spots until I find a place where it produces a more resonant thump and then start banging that place. Daniel keeps waving the improvised flag on his own, resting often to catch his breath.

We're both sweating after a few minutes. I want to throw up, but there's nothing in my stomach. The sail is getting closer. And it is a sail. Definitely a sail. I can see it's four-sided, a kind of rig I can't remember the name of. Jonathan would know. Jonathan...

I shake my head, try to focus. I stand up again and start banging on the barrel with as much strength as I can muster. Daniel takes the pillowcase off the oar and waves it back and forth in his hands. If they're paying attention, we will surely catch the eye and ear of whoever's in the boat.

It looks like a small vessel. Maybe just a canoe with a sail on it. Or a rowboat? But who would be out on Georgian Bay in such a small boat? Could it be another lifeboat from the *Asia*? One with a sail?

The boat tacks away from us. "Helllp! Heeeelp us!" Daniel shouts frantically.

It keeps moving away while we shout and bang and wave our ridiculous flag.

My voice is a croak, my arms like anvils. We're both dripping with sweat when the sail finally flips back onto the other side. They're headed in our direction again, and we cheer. "Over here! Over here!" Daniel shouts as I join in.

Even when it's clear the boat is definitely headed to our shore, we refuse to stop.

Thirteen

I think they're Indians. A man at the helm, a woman tending the sail. Both of them have long, nearly black hair. They're speaking to one another as they pull up to the shore, angling their boat into a sheltered bay a few hundred feet from where we're yelling and jumping. Their boat is small, wooden, pointy at the ends, as if it is part canoe but with two masts and a small jib. They drop the sails away from shore, folding them quickly inside the boat.

I've never spoken to an Indian before. Not directly anyway. People from the nearby reserve come in regularly to Owen Sound to sell fish and buy things, to plead their case against the Indian agent. Once, when I was younger, I was with my cousins and brother on the dock when two canoes full of Indian children arrived. The boys were dressed in breechcloth and leather leggings, the girls draped in blankets. They ranged in age from a toddler to a boy my age. They stared at us, and my cousins and brother and I stared back.

Then Jonathan made everyone laugh by pretending to fall on a loose plank in the government dock. We all giggled at him together, as if we were classmates or neighbors or friends. It was nothing, really, no more than a few seconds. But it made me wonder not just about what they were wearing, how different they were from us, but also how much we might share—laughing at the same things, spending time with cousins and friends—and what *they* might think of me, of us, of white people.

It was strange and new to think such a thing, and seeing this couple tying up their boat reminds me of this. It reminds me, too, of how in these last few days so many things I'd once thought were undeniable have turned out to be false.

But what if this couple doesn't speak English? What if we can't explain what's happened to us? What if they won't help us? I look over at Daniel, but he's already running down toward the boat. I scramble to catch up.

"Hello!" he calls. "Hello! We need help. We're shipwrecked. We survived a shipwreck." He flings his arm toward the open bay.

The man approaches us. He's tall, with a sharp chin and high cheekbones. He's wearing clothes like my father might on a fishing trip—dark, crumpled pants and a button-up shirt with suspenders. His pants are loose at the waist, and he's put on a bowler hat that he wears high on his head. He holds up a hand in greeting, but there's nothing in his face that makes me think he understands our desperation.

Daniel tries speaking more calmly this time. "Our ship went down in a storm. The *Asia*. We're the only survivors." He points to the lifeboat.

The woman appears behind the man. She is small, with large dark eyes and unlined skin, older than me but perhaps not by much. She wears a long black skirt and a striped shirt-waist, a blanket like a heavy shawl around her shoulders. She shrugs it off and hands her blanket to me, then says something I don't understand.

I try to say thank you, but my lips feel loose. I pull the stiff blanket around my shoulders and shiver from head to toe.

"Come," the man says and gestures with his hand toward the water.

Daniel looks down at his gold watch, the one he's been fiddling with every time we have a quiet moment. He pauses, then takes it off quickly and hands it to the man. "Could you take us to Parry Sound? Please? Parry Sound?"

The man shrugs and takes the watch. He says something to the woman, and they both walk toward their boat.

I lean in toward Daniel. "Do they understand?" I whisper.

"I think so," he says.

"She gave me her blanket," I say.

"Exactly. Why would we be here with no food or shelter if we aren't in trouble?" he says.

"You think it's safe?" I ask.

Daniel looks at me with his eyebrows raised. "Safe? As opposed to staying on an island on the edge of the bay with no food or shelter?"

"Right."

"We're going to be okay," he says, picking up my hand and squeezing it. "We better go."

We follow the couple toward their boat until Daniel stops and calls out, "The lifeboat!" He points to it banging against the shore.

The man nods his head. "Yes," he says and gestures to Daniel to bring it around to him.

I follow the woman. She leans into their boat and pulls a rough woven cloth off a basket heavy with blackberries. She holds the basket up and hands it to me, speaking softly. "*Odatagaagominag.*"

My mouth suddenly aches in anticipation of the tangy fruit. And yet, after not eating for two days, I'm not sure I can hold anything down. I don't want to insult our rescuers, so I take two and put them in my mouth. She gestures that I should have more. I nod and smile, holding the berries in my hand. When Daniel has pulled our lifeboat along the shore and handed the lifeline over, the woman offers some to him as well.

The blackberries are plump and sweet. Daniel and I stand there immobilized, chewing, swallowing, like we've never eaten such a delicacy before. I savor the taste, rolling the seeds around in my mouth. They are more citrusy than I recall; their seeds stick in my teeth. The juice stains my hand.

"Let's go," the man says impatiently. "To Parry Sound." The woman says a few sharp words to him and puts a firm hand on his shoulder. He straightens up.

"Yes," both of us say.

"Parry Sound. Thank you," I add.

I step into the boat first. The woman directs me to sit on the wooden floor, and I collapse into a heap. There are many of those same woven baskets and other containers made of birchbark. Some overflow with mushrooms, others with more blackberries, a few with cranberries. I huddle beneath the blanket she's given me. I'm shaking, though I'm not sure if it's from relief or fear or the cold.

Just before Daniel gets in, I see his face change, as if he's seen something. My heart leaps into my mouth.

"Wait!" he calls as he turns to run back toward the point. "I'll just be a second."

The three of us watch him in confusion. The woman looks at me and I shrug, holding up my hands. Daniel runs along the shore, his coat flapping behind him, then up the rocky slope toward the barrel. He disappears for a second, and we hear him call out. "I'm still here!"

He's soon back up where we can see him, and he hoists the pillowcase in the air.

When he returns Daniel is directed toward the back of the boat. We push off, and the woman takes the oars, steering us away from shore.

Already I can sense the roll of the waves from the open water coming down the channel. The man hands me some salted meat, and I gnaw on it to be polite, but I'm not sure I can swallow.

The breeze is crisp, and I tug the woman's blanket over my shoulders. The waves out in the open look big. There is nothing but water. Nothing but the wreckage of the *Asia*, the wreckage of all those lives. I shake my head to rid myself of the image of the bodies we buried, the grave we made. But just when I'm starting to think I have to say something, tell them I can't bear to be out there in the big water again, the woman turns our small boat inland.

"Where are we going?" Daniel asks from the stern. He leans over, speaking to our rescuer urgently. I can't hear what they're saying, but I see the man point toward the lifeboat we're towing behind us. Daniel nods and sits back down.

"We're going to drop it off," Daniel calls to me, gesturing toward the lifeboat with his head. "It's all right," he says and places his right hand over his chest. I can almost feel the pressure over my own heart.

The woman turns around and glances toward me. She says something softly, holding one hand up to her ear and tilting her head, closing her eyes—*sleep*—then adds something I don't understand.

The breeze is good in the wide inland channel, and the man and woman work together to put up their sail. Soon we're moving along quickly. I look behind us at the waves our boat creates, tiny ripcurls surging on either side. The boat is low in the water, stable. We roll softly back and forth with the wind. It's soothing, like the gentle movement of a rumbling train, and I close my eyes. I'm asleep in seconds.

❖　　❖　　❖

Smoke rises up over the dense green shore in the distance. The sun is already past its highest point. It's less windy here, and the islands are close. I've been sleeping since we set out. It looks like Daniel has too. I can see him stirring at the back of the boat, his eyes puffy, his face creased with sleep.

He's down low, tucked under the wooden gunnels, and looks smaller and younger than before.

I feel safe under the blanket with the blackberries and mushrooms, the boat rocking with the wind. But as we tuck behind a larger island, the breeze dies. The couple drops the sails quickly once again, an operation as smooth and efficient as sliding a card into an envelope.

"*Shawanaga*," the man says to us and points toward a break in the shoreline up ahead.

I don't understand and look toward Daniel. "The river," he says.

When we turn in, the wind of the bay is silenced altogether. It's utterly calm. The water takes on the dark, green reflection of the pine and cedar trees that grow close on both sides. *As green as em-er-ald,* I think to myself. Here and there the woman takes a sharp turn with her oars to avoid shoals or half-submerged logs that pop out of the water.

We enter a wider portion of the river, and up ahead I can see smoke and smell wood burning, though I don't see anyone. The river seems to end in a wide bay. Closest to us there's a small chute that burbles down over large rocks. A rough wooden dam holds up the shore beside it. The couple pulls up to a marshy area, and the man gets out, untying our lifeboat and guiding it into a swampy cove. Daniel joins him, stepping into water up to his knees, and helps pull the bow of the heavy metal boat onto solid ground.

The woman rows us over to some rocks and steps out too, stretching her legs and encouraging me to do the same. For the first time, I notice that under her skirt she's wearing soft leather moccasins embroidered with a few tiny, colorful beads. We stand close together in silence.

"*Odatagaagominag,*" she says, offering me more berries. This time I can't get enough.

"Oda-ta..." I try once I've had my fill.

She laughs. "*Odatagaagominag.*"

"O-ta-ta-gaa-go..."

She shakes her head and waves her hand for me to stop. She tries sounding it out for me slowly, but I bungle it over and over. We both laugh.

I can see Daniel and the Indian man just out of earshot, both talking with their hands. The man turns and walks away. When he comes back there are two other Indian men with him. They glance toward us and nod. The four of them pull the lifeboat up so it's completely out of the water and then the two men disappear into the woods.

When Daniel returns to us, his cheeks are flushed. "He said we can't make it to Parry Sound tonight." He looks down into the boat. "I'm sorry."

"So we'll stay here?" I can't keep the disappointment from my voice. I feel something in my throat, a protest, an ache.

"No. We'll leave the lifeboat here. We can make better time without it. He said we'll stay somewhere farther south. I didn't understand everything."

I look at the woman, and she nods. She has been so kind to me, and I don't even know her name.

"Christina," I say, touching my chest. "Daniel," I say, pointing toward him.

"Eva," she says, doing the same.

I'm surprised to hear she has a Christian name, though I know missionaries have been coming up along this shore for years.

"Henry," she says, pointing at the man, who's headed back toward our boat.

We soon set off again, back out the long river and into a wide inlet where we can put the sail up. Being in the boat again makes me sleepy. This time I try to fight it, but I can't. In fact, I find myself going deep, as if pressed underwater. I sink down into the shadowy depths where there is no sound, no light. Nothing.

❖   ❖   ❖

There's a cool hand on my forehead. Eva's face is close, blurry like it's been painted with watercolors. I'm hot, stifled, beneath the blanket. It feels like being cooped up inside our airless house on a still August night. I throw the blanket off my shoulders and try to sit up.

"No," Eva says pressing me down firmly. "Sleep."

These are some of the first words Eva has spoken that I know. I'm not sure if I'm more surprised by this or the fact that I am no longer in the boat but lying on a rock some distance from the water.

"Fever," she says.

I look around, my eyes adjusting to the light. The sun is dipping lower in the sky. Eva is right beside me. I can see Daniel sitting by the water with his back to us. His shoulders are sloped, neck bent. I don't see Henry at all.

"Where are we?" I ask.

Eva's eyes are tender. "*Mshiikenh-zhiibigweshing*," she says. "Turtle."

Daniel hears us talking and comes over, dropping to his knees beside me. "Are you all right? You had me frightened. You were calling out in the boat," he says. "A dream. *Why me?* you said. I think you have a fever."

"Where's the turtle?" I ask.

Daniel extends an arm along the shore. "It's a big rock shaped like a turtle's head," he explains. "Henry is offering tobacco. For safe passage."

"Sleep," Eva says, stroking my forehead. She unwraps a leather bundle tied with a cord that sits in her lap. Inside are twisted pieces of grass and a pile of what look like thin, dark sticks all in a tangle. She snaps off a piece of one of the sticks and gives it to me.

"Fever," she says when she sees my hesitation. She mimes putting it in her mouth and chewing.

I search Eva's face for more, but she just nods encouragingly. Her hair blows in front of her face, and she tucks it back behind her ears, then with both hands laces it effortlessly into a braid that goes down her back. I didn't notice before how beautiful she is. I wonder if she's Henry's wife. Or maybe a sister, a mother with children of her own? I don't know what it is, but something about Eva makes me feel safe.

I put the stick in my mouth and bite down. It tastes surprisingly like ginger, a bit spicy but without the sharpness. I wrinkle my forehead in confusion, and Eva smiles.

I work on chewing the stick while she and Daniel watch me. The flavor fades, but the stick is woody and turns to fibers in my mouth. When Eva is distracted by Henry's return, I spit the last bits onto the rock.

"Let's go," Henry says.

Daniel pushes himself to his feet.

But Eva makes no effort to move. She continues to stroke my forehead, and I feel calmness invade my body. I'm starting to sweat, and I drift off again, sinking, sinking. This time I don't fight it.

The next thing I know, we're pulling into a new place, the sky still light but the sun gone from view. Eva and Daniel help me from the boat and prop me against a rock in the shelter of a pine tree while they set up camp. My forehead is damp, my dress soaked through, but I no longer feel hot, just muddled and exhausted. Daniel helps Eva and Henry craft a shelter out of nothing—twigs and branches, a hide of something that looks like deer. I must be feverish still, because I see a bird helping them, a seagull carrying ribbons of dried grasses. Eva tries to give me something to drink, her fingers prying my lips open, but I turn my head, tighten my jaw, refuse. My throat is too sore to swallow.

Morning is upon us before I even know I have slept. We start out again as soon as the wind begins. Daniel helps me to the boat, his eyes worried, forehead wrinkled. It takes too much effort to form words, and I just shake my head when he tries to speak to me.

The haze that fills my mind begins to lift with the sun. When we turn into the shelter of Parry Sound, I can see the town rising up from the water like a stage set. A mill, a smokestack, a ravaged hill denuded of trees, pockmarked with exposed rock and tree stumps. Tiny figures moving about on the docks.

I remember arriving here on the steamer with Jonathan. There were fewer buildings then, more trees. We were excited to see a town after an afternoon and night in the solitude of the open water. The mate promised hand-cranked ice cream at the general store near the docks—*best in the east*, he said.

Today I feel only dread. I'm sweating again—my cheeks are flushed. I thought I would feel relieved to be back in civilization, to be rescued from certain death, but instead, seeing the town and the men rushing about on the dock, the boats and sails and horse-drawn wagons, I'm struck again by what we have just endured. I want to find Daniel, see his face, know that he remembers too, but he's tunneled down beneath the blankets like a mole.

"Parry Sound," Henry calls out, and I see the blankets covering Daniel begin to stir.

Along the shore, lumber is stacked in piles as high as a schooner. It looks like a pencil drawing done with a ruler—perfect, straight lines. Boats, most of them small, meant for fishing, dot the bay here and there. Some are tied up at dock; others are anchored in the water just past the river. The chimney stacks of houses and large wood-frame buildings whisper smoky murmurs into the sky.

I hear the *hwah* of a seagull and look up, hoping absurdly to see the bird from the other day. But there are many seagulls, all of them flying around like tugboats escorting a ship into harbor.

The wind begins to die as we get closer, and Henry and Eva set to work dousing the sails. I want to help them, show my gratitude, but when I try to move, the muscles in my legs are putty, my head a spinning top. Eva looks at me with eyebrows raised and shakes her head no. She points to the bottom of the boat. I should sit.

Henry and Eva fold the sails and get out oars. We are bumping up against the stone-filled cribs of a large, wide dock within minutes.

I watch the men on the docks with their untamed beards and callused hands, their frayed wool pants and faded hats. They are young and old and move about like a kind of machine, few of them speaking but working together without need of words. Moving cargo, hauling wood, cleaning boats. Picking up, passing, carrying. I hear one call to another in French, someone respond in English. A thick-necked tabby cat sneaks down the dock, sniffing here and there. It rubs its long orange-and-white striped side along one burly man's boot. The man reaches down and scratches the old cat behind its ear, and it leans in toward him.

These men pay us little attention until we are banging up against the high dock. Their faces flicker with confusion, then disbelief as Daniel calls out, "We were on the *Asia*. The boat is sunk. We are survivors! Help us." He holds up the pillowcase with *S.S. Asia* stenciled along the hem.

There's a moment in which nothing happens, as if no one can quite believe what he is hearing. Then one man shouts, "Survivors!" and scrambles to take the bowline. Another reaches far down into the boat to haul Daniel up like a fish on a line. They gesture to me. "*Petite fille*," they gasp. I lift my arms, and someone takes my hands. The blanket falls from my shoulders as I'm in the air. "A girl," one says. "A child."

I don't have time to think about how strange these words sound, how little I feel like a child, before I am half carried, half dragged down the dock, men smelling of sweat and wood and coal pushing in on either side of me. I am still weak, my forehead on fire once again, and I let them lift me, though I don't like their arms around my waist, though I want to turn back to Eva to say, *Thank you, thank you for your berries and your kindness. Thank you, Henry, for keeping us safe when there was no one else.* Daniel is beside me, though he is allowed to walk on his own. I can hear him talking to the men, but I can't make out the words. There are shouts all around us. "The *Asia!* Survivors! Make way! Survivors!"

I am carried to a building not far from the docks. Before I go inside, I insist on turning back toward the water. I can see the two masts of Henry and Eva's little boat. They are at the edge of the harbor, oars out, disappearing into the sky.

Fourteen

Days have passed without me knowing the sun from the moon, light from dark. There have been doctors and a girl to wipe my fevered forehead and spoon hot broth into my mouth. I know I've been having dreams about snakes and waves and a seagull that lets me fly on its back, my knees tucked in close to its wings. I have called out. Cried for help, for release. There have been curious children who've come to look at me and been shooed away. I have seen their eyes at the door, heard their tiny footsteps running away. I've heard snatches of conversation too: *rescue, search party, Indians, debris, coffin ship.* But there is nothing I can form into a coherent idea, a thought, nothing I can form into an urge to get out of this bed.

One evening as the lowering sun is casting shadows around the hotel room, a young man not much older than me slips into my room and shuts the door behind him. I don't know him, can barely see his face in the low light. He approaches my bed, and I gasp when he puts a finger to his lips and whispers that we don't have much time. I must explain my story to him. He is a reporter from Toronto. He has spoken to the boy, Mr. Thompson, he says, but needs my side of the tragic tale. The public has the right to know. Someone must be held responsible. More than a hundred souls lost.

His voice grows louder as he peppers me with questions. *Was the captain drunk? Is it true he couldn't even read? Who died first? How did they die? Where did you leave the bodies? Did the Indians who brought you to Parry Sound demand a gold watch in payment for safe passage? Is it true that Daniel Thompson saved you, that you would have died without him? Is it true that you fell in love out there?*

I hear the man's intention, see the urgency in his darting eyes, but it is all a jumble, like a familiar word you see written down that looks suddenly like a foreign language. I turn from him. "Go," I say, pulling the blankets around me. "Leave me alone."

He protests and I try to ignore him, burrow down into that dark place outside time and space where I have lived these last few days. But he persists. He puts his hand on my shoulder, and I begin to shout just as the doctor flings open the door, light rushing in. The girl who watches me is close at his heels. She shoots a nervous look at the reporter. "Get out!" the doctor shouts. "She's a child, for God's sake! Have pity, you wretch! Get out!"

The young man walks slowly, deliberately, giving a broad wink to the servant girl as he leaves.

"And you!" the doctor says to the girl with a hiss. "You're finished here." He points an outstretched arm toward the door.

She looks down in embarrassment and quickly leaves the room.

The man pulls a chair up beside my bed, setting an oil lamp down on a small table. "I'm Dr. Roberts," he says gently. He takes off his spectacles and cleans them with the front of his shirt. The glasses have left an indent on the top of his nose. He rubs the skin there before putting them back on. "I'm sorry about that. The newspapers are rabid for your story. Parry Sound is crawling with reporters. There's an inquest being held. Mr. Thompson has already spoken to them. He told a terrible tale."

My mouth is dry. "I don't understand."

Dr. Roberts pours me a glass of water from a pitcher on a nearby dressing table. The cold liquid burns my throat.

"Newspapers," the doctor explains. "They want to know what happened to the *Asia*, to him, to both of you. How the others died. I imagine that scoundrel asked you about romance. I'm sorry about that. So improper. But the rags are creating quite the story of star-crossed lovers. A fairy tale." The doctor winks, and I feel heat rising up my neck.

"Don't worry yourself. Mr. Thompson wouldn't say anything untoward. He spoke highly of your resources, your kindness to him. He said you were brave and good, that you helped the men keep up their spirits, that you held the mate in your arms as he died, that you offered comfort to the captain as he breathed his last. Mr. Thompson said you saved his life too."

I turn my head on the pillow and swallow back the tears. *Brave. Kind. Good.* I have never heard such words used to describe me. Jonathan, yes, but not me. I don't know what to think. I don't know how to feel. Everything that happened out there with Daniel is like another life, another me.

"This is not going to be easy, Miss McBurney," the doctor continues. "You should know that from the outset. Not easy at all. There are people who will want things from you. Reporters. Government officials. Police, possibly. Men from the shipping company. I feel, as your physician, that I need to warn you. You must be prepared. You must be strong."

I rub my face. I haven't thought about any of this.

"I'll try to protect you as best I can," the doctor says. "But once you're well again, my job will be done. You're going to have to shore yourself up. This story is the biggest news in the country, and you and Mr. Thompson, well, everyone wants to know how you survived when so many didn't."

I suddenly have a terrifying thought. What if one of those reporters decides to dig into Daniel's past, his uncle's business dealings? If Daniel's name is connected to the scam, he could be arrested. And, perhaps worse, what if his uncle survived?

"Have any others been found? Survivors?" I ask.

Dr. Roberts shakes his head. "I'm afraid not. It's just you and Mr. Thompson." He swallows, speaking sternly now. "He's stubborn, that boy. I can hardly hold him back from going to help the search parties. He says the two of you marked the spot on the shore where you left the men's bodies. He wants to help find them, give them a proper burial. He's quite insistent. But he's not ready. Not yet."

"Is he unwell?"

"His body is recovering. That bump on his head was nasty, and he still has headaches, but that's to be expected. He remembers most everything now except how he hit his head.

But it's the trauma of the thing, you see. Going back to the site, et cetera. I don't think he's quite ready for all that." The doctor stands up, readjusts his glasses.

"You've had a fright. A terrible scare. Both of you. It affects a person. Changes a person, I believe."

He leans down and pulls the blanket up to my neck, tucking my arms in as if I'm an infant. I let him because I am too overwhelmed to argue.

"You've asked for him, you know. Many times. I'll arrange it when you're well enough. But for now, you rest. Doctor's orders." He winks again.

"But," I say, unconvincingly, "I'm better. Truly. I need to see Daniel. I need to speak to him."

The doctor pauses, his hand on the doorknob. "You might be better, but you're not well yet. Not tip-top, which you'll have to be to face the hordes. Trust me. Mr. Thompson is not going anywhere. Not if I have anything to say about it." He tugs on his suspenders, does up the front button of his coat. "You won't be disturbed again."

I sink back into the bed and glance around at the dark wallpaper and heavy furniture. The door clicks closed. It's quiet, but my mind is in flight. I flip through everything that's happened like wind riffling the pages of a book. A lifetime packed into those few days. The doctor is right. I am changed.

I roll back and forth, twisting myself up in the sheets until I have to pull them all off and start again. I can't get comfortable. I am tired but can't sleep. I walk over to the window and feel exhausted almost immediately. The wooden floor is freezing beneath my bare feet. I have to sit down on a small hard chair, tuck my feet up, pull the flannel nightshirt over my legs. I cringe to think that I don't even remember putting the nightshirt on myself.

The hotel is up a small rise with a view of the harbor. It's too dark to see much in the distance other than the outline of the shore, though I can also make out vague shadows of boats large and small bobbing at anchor or tied to the docks. Candles flicker in windows. Across the road, wind whips a flag flying at half-mast, and I think of all the mothers and fathers and sons, the sisters and uncles and brothers who lost their loved ones on the *Asia*. I think of the women in my stateroom, the mother with two children I could not save, my cousin, the captain, the cabin boy, the men in our lifeboat. Even Daniel's uncle might have someone who will miss him, someone who will mark his life with a stone or flowers or song. I hug my legs close and press my eyes against the hard bone of my knees, trying not to see their faces, hear their shouts, their cries and dying prayers. I will never know why I survived and they did not.

I sit like that for a long time, and just when it seems the entire village is asleep, the horn of a steamer rounding the point bounces off the rock and echoes around the harbor. I peer out again and see a boat moving quickly through the pitch, the pilothouse and stern aglow with oil lamps. It's one of the smaller steamers, like those I've seen at dock in Owen Sound, a workboat maybe. I hear the whistle calling men to bring it in. A horse and wagon flies by the hotel at top speed, so close I can hear the crunch of the animal's hooves, the wheels grinding the hard-packed ground beneath my window. Maybe it's a search boat. Maybe something or someone has been found.

I think about the doctor's warning, how there will be many people who want something from me. The very idea of it makes me more tired. How would I know why the boat sank, why we survived, if someone was at fault? Not even the captain seemed to know what actually happened that terrible morning.

I drift in and out on the hard chair. A voice jolts me awake. "Christina?"

There's a figure at the door. I'm about to call out, raise the alarm, when I realize it's a woman. Mother.

"Darling," she says, speaking in a quiet voice, her words directed toward the bed, where blankets piled in a heap look like a person under covers. She opens the door, and light from the hallway rushes into the room. Her hand goes up to her mouth. She is wearing a thick black coat and long knitted scarf, a hat pulled low around her face. I can see the deeply carved lines around her mouth, dark circles beneath her eyes.

"Here," I say, and she gasps.

"Oh, Chris," she says, rushing to my side. "Darling. I've been so worried." She kneels on the ground by my chair and drapes her head over my legs. "We thought...we thought... we thought you were gone too."

She looks back up at me and begins to sob. I raise my hand to touch her, then pause. I ran away. She will be furious. But she drops her head into my lap again and cries inconsolably. I place my hand on her shoulder, rub back and forth, wanting to say something but unable to speak.

"Why, Christina? Why?" she asks eventually, looking up at me, her face stained with tears. "Why did you run away? After everything we've been through?"

"I'm sorry," I say. "I'm sorry. I should never have left without telling you."

She searches my face, surprised by my quick apology.

"I've been looking for him," I say, choking back the boulder in my throat. "Some flicker of his presence, his voice, his touch. I lost...I lost half of myself when he died. I don't know how to be without him...without Jonathan."

Mother flinches at the sound of his name. She shakes her head, looking down at the rough pine floors.

"I don't either, darling. None of us do." She looks back at me, then stands up and wraps her arms firmly around my back. I lean toward her, melt into her body. I don't remember the last time she hugged me like this, and I'm not going to let go.

Eventually she releases me. "Thank God for the quick thinking of your dear cousin," she says. "Peter sent off a telegram the night you sailed. Told us you were with him, that he'd...that he'd look after you." She dissolves into tears again.

"Poor Mary," she sobs. "Those orphaned children. And my sister. Well, she's had to be sedated. I think she's still hoping... against hope..."

I shake my head glumly.

Mother looks away, wipes her eyes, then unpins her hat and pulls it off, adjusting her hair absentmindedly, tucking and poking it back into place. She drags another wooden chair over beside me.

"I left Parkdale before we heard about the wreck," she says. "The morning I got Peter's telegram. I was angry. I won't pretend otherwise. I thought I'd drag you back home kicking and screaming if necessary. But then I arrived in Owen Sound and no steamers were leaving because of the storm."

She takes one of my hands in both of hers, cupping it inside.

"I had to wait a few days, and still no one would go out. At first people said the *Asia* would have tucked in somewhere and was riding out the storm." She sighs, shakes her head.

"Then, when there was no word from anywhere up and down the bay, they told me to prepare for the worst. I thought—I thought you were dead. I heard the news just yesterday. I took the only boat out."

My mother chasing me around Georgian Bay seems so unlikely, I don't know what to make of it. She's stopped crying, but her eyes are rimmed with red as she stares toward the door.

"We picked up a body from the *Asia* on the way here. Some debris too." She fishes a handkerchief from her pocket and wipes her eyes again, blows her nose. She breathes deeply and places my hand back in my own lap.

I am freezing all of a sudden and hug my arms around myself.

"I'm so sorry," I offer again.

"I know," she says gently, and it makes me wonder if I know my own mother at all. "I know you are, my darling girl."

❖   ❖   ❖

Another horn from the docks wakes me just as the sun is cracking open the sky. I lie in bed and watch the horizon begin to glow. I must have slept, because I feel stronger, my thoughts less cloudy.

Before I went to sleep, I told Mother about the wreck and the lifeboat, about Peter and the captain, Eva and Henry and the turtle. I left out the parts she doesn't need to know. The parts that I still don't understand myself. She listened intently, grasping my hand when my voice cracked, then held me and rubbed my back when I was finished. I fell asleep like that. I woke when I heard her leave much later, though she tiptoed on the creaky floor.

I glance around the hotel room again. The dress I was wearing on the ship is hanging on a hook by the window. It looks as if it's been cleaned, mended, ironed. I don't see the holes and tears or the blood and dirt I remember. Peter's logbook is on the table beside my bed, the pages buckled and swollen. I pick it up to read again, and the studio photograph falls onto my lap. Those sweet, trusting faces, those lives that will never be the same again. I slip it back inside and tuck down into bed, facing the door, trying not to think about returning the book to Mary, passing on her husband's final words.

I'm wrapped up in these thoughts when there's a gentle knock. The door swings open. Daniel puts a finger to his lips and mouths *shshshshsh*, then turns his back to press the door closed quietly.

"You scared me," I say, my voice raspy.

"Sorry," he says, looking down at the floor, suddenly bashful. "But they wouldn't let me see you and, well, I'm leaving." He stands close enough that I can hear his low voice, far enough away that I can't touch him if I wanted to. If I thought he wanted it. If I knew what I wanted.

"What? Really? When?"

He fingers the buttons of his jacket. "Now. I'm going with the *Northern Belle* to look for wreckage, to show them the bodies."

"The doctor told me he thinks you aren't ready. He says you shouldn't go. It will be too traumatic or something."

"Yeah, well, I'm the one who gets to decide that, right?" He clears his throat, straightens up, as if trying to look taller.

I'm surprised by the tone of his voice. It's like he's talking to someone else, someone who didn't just survive the unsurvivable with him. I want to remind him who I am, what we lived through. But something stops me. Something in the way he holds his shoulders, his hands clenched firmly in front of him. I pat the blanket down over my legs, adjust my tight braids.

"A chair," I say. "There's one by the window."

I watch as he carries it over. His jacket is new-looking, the white shirt underneath pressed and clean. His hair is combed. He looks different, less thin and pointy, less tired, though there's something familiar too. I have to hold one hand in the other so I don't reach out to him.

"How are you feeling?" he asks. "The doctor made it sound as if you've barely been clinging to life. Fevers. Hallucinations. But you look fine to me—uh, I mean, you look better than the last time I saw you. I mean...you look well."

"Thanks." I shrug. There's an awkward silence, and I rush to fill it. "So you're going to look for...for the men?"

Daniel nods grimly. "I want them to be brought home. They have to be brought home. It's the least I can do. Their families, you know. And I...we...know where they are. That whole shoreline is engraved in my mind. I think I could create a map of every nook and bay, every inlet and shoal that we saw."

I nod, though I can't say the same. Each tree is like the next, each rock as sharp and cruel as pointy teeth. I don't want to go there again—ever. I pick at a loose thread on the blanket.

"But…well…Chris…I mean, Christina, Miss McBurney…"
I shake my head. *Miss McBurney?* But he keeps talking.

"What I really want is to say thank you. You saved me.
I wouldn't have survived without you. Not just when I hit my
head. I still don't know how you pulled me back into the boat.
I've heard of people having superhuman strength in terrible
moments, but…it wasn't just that. It was also you talking to
me. Telling me about your brother. Letting me tell you, *forcing
me*"—he grins—"to tell you about my uncle. I know I didn't
want to, but, well…I'm just glad you were there."

Me too, me too, I scream inside my head.

Daniel straightens up again, puts his lips together and
twists his neck back and forth, pulling at his collar as if it's
too tight. "I also need to ask a favor."

What could I possibly do for him? I can barely stand or
speak. I can't even say thank you. "Of course," I say.

Daniel leans in, his voice quiet. "I need you to not tell
anyone about my uncle. The advert, his lies. The fraud. It's
serious. It *could* be serious." He rubs his face with his hands,
then looks at me earnestly. "I promise you, I'll make it right
with the people he tricked. I'll give them their money back,
even if I have to sell the store. I want to wash my hands
of him. Of that. I just want to be an honest shopkeeper.
An honest man."

"Of course," I say, pulling my hands out from underneath
the blanket. "Of course. You don't even have to ask. I won't
breathe a word."

He looks so relieved, I nearly laugh out loud.

"There you go again," he says, grinning. "Laughing at
things that aren't funny."

I reach out to him, and we grasp each other's hand. His is cool and dry and fits perfectly in mine. We sit there for a second, and I'm flooded with sadness and hope, and I have no idea what it means.

He leans in and whispers. "We're going to be okay," he says.

"Promise?" I ask with a smile.

"Christina?"

Daniel and I both jump, pulling our hands back.

My mother is standing at the door, her back straight, her mouth severe. "Mother," I say a little too quickly. "I didn't hear you come in. This is Daniel. Daniel Thompson. The other...the other survivor."

Daniel stands up, holding his hat in his hand. "Pleased to meet you, Mrs. McBurney."

"Oh," Mother says stiffly. "Young man, I think...I think you'd better go. You shouldn't be here...alone...unchaperoned..." She looks behind her. "This is most unusual."

"I'm sorry," Daniel says. "I shouldn't have come. Don't be angry with Christina. It's my fault. I was just saying goodbye. I had to. Say goodbye, I mean. I'm leaving. I'll go now."

No, I want to say. *Don't go. Please. Don't go.* He offers his hand for me to shake, and I take it firmly, as if to telegraph my regret. "Thank you, Miss McBurney," he says. The words catch, and he clears his throat. "Goodbye, Christina." He loosens his grip.

But I don't. I won't. "Thank *you*, Daniel," I say, looking him straight in the eyes. "We made each other better. I won't forget that. You. I won't forget you."

Daniel's eyes stay locked on mine. He nods slowly once, then drops my hand. He smiles and gently presses on his chest above his heart before slipping out the door.

Mother follows Daniel into the hallway to make sure he's gone, then steps back inside. I don't know if I'll ever see Daniel again, and it makes me feel as tired as I did on the lifeboat and that rocky, desolate shore. I've only known him a few days, and yet I feel as if we are ancient creatures who recognized each other from another time.

This version of me that he described, this person who helped him, who showed courage, who made him feel less alone, is one I still don't entirely recognize. It isn't the story my parents have told or even the one I have told about myself. But it is me. A kinder, gentler, sadder, braver, twinless me. And right now, it feels about as true as anything else. Perhaps I am all of those things and other things too. Other things I don't even know about yet.

"Darling," Mother says, "I'm sorry to chase him away like that. I just..."

"I know, Mother. I just need a minute." She looks as if she is about to object, but then nods and leaves me, closing the door firmly behind her. I slide back down under the blanket, my face still exposed. I feel my weight sink into the bed. I am heavy, and I imagine the outline of my body making a deep impression on the hard mattress.

I can see another flagpole, the flag at half-mast. Jonathan died, but I did not. The others from the *Asia* are gone, but Daniel and I survived. We are survivors.

I don't know what's in store for me now. What I will be, what I will become. But I know now that I am large. I contain big water, big sky. For I have held a person in my arms as he died, found solace in the wind and sky, scared away wild animals with laughter. I have watched kindness and determination and grief exist at the same time in the same face. Maybe I will forge my own path, like Daniel said. Become a scientist or a teacher. Or maybe I'll marry a farmer and live a quiet life in a quiet town and have babies and grandbabies, make jam in the summer and pickles in the fall. Maybe I'll travel the ocean, or maybe I'll never set another foot on a boat. I might never again hold someone's hand and face the unknown together, frightened and defiant and alive. Or I might. I just might.

Author's note

This book is based on the true story of the wreck of the steamship *Asia*, but it is fiction. I have changed names and details, created backstories and conversations, and inserted characters wholesale from my imagination, though I have tried to remain true to the period and basic outline of the ship's last voyage. It is my sincerest hope that in my imagining, I have honored the real-life survivors as well as those lost in this disaster and the many other wrecks on the Great Lakes.

Shipwrecks were, sadly, quite common on Georgian Bay in the late-nineteenth and early-twentieth centuries. Without proper maps, travel by water was dangerous but also necessary, as there were not yet many roads or trains traveling to the region.

But the terrible loss of the *Asia* was different. Stories about the disaster were plastered across the front pages of newspapers around the country. Firsthand accounts from the survivors thrilled and horrified the public. Poems and songs were written. Two independent investigations into the causes of the wreck were held. The result was lots of speculation but no definitive answer about what happened.

The site of the wreck has still not been discovered. Many people blamed the captain's poor judgment in leaving port when a storm was forecast. Others believed that the *Asia*, built high and narrow to fit through canals, was unsuited to travel on the open water. Others said that such high winds and waves would topple any steamer. Some suggest it was a combination of all of these factors. There were other people who believed she might have hit an unmarked shoal.

One good thing did come out of the foundering of the SS *Asia*: the public outcry pushed the Government of Canada to commission the Georgian Bay Survey, a nautical mapping of the treacherous waters. Starting in the summer of 1883, the survey took eleven long, painstaking seasons to complete. After the bay was properly mapped, the number of shipwrecks began to decrease.

You've probably noticed that the main characters in the novel use the word *Indians* to describe the First Nations people who appear in the book. This was common in 1882, but even then it was a misnomer, a word used by the earliest European explorers who mistakenly believed they'd landed in India. Over the years, the word *Indian* became associated with the damaging colonizing policies of the Canadian government toward Indigenous people, and it is used rarely today.

The couple in the book were likely Anishinaabeg from the shores of eastern Georgian Bay. I have used Ojibwe words that they might have used, including *Mshiikenh-zhiibigweshing* for the great stone turtle where they stop to offer tobacco. According to scholar Brian McInnes, writing in *Sounding Thunder: The Stories of Francis Pegahmagabow*, about the celebrated WWI sniper from the Wasauksing First

Nation near Parry Sound, it means "turtle lying there with his neck extended."

It is worthwhile to note that in the contemporary reporting on the wreck, the First Nations' rescuers were not named or their significant help truly acknowledged. In fact, it was suggested that the couple demanded the gold watch for their troubles and were reluctant to assist the teenagers. I found this highly unlikely. As I discovered in my research, newspapers at the time commonly employed racist stereotypes and cast aspersions on the motives and actions of First Nations people. Thank you to Waubgeshig Rice, a talented author and journalist from the Wasauksing First Nation, who read this section of *Big Water* to help ensure that the dignity of his people is honored in these pages, as it was so often not in 1882.

Acknowledgments

After writing my first book about a Georgian Bay shipwreck, I thought I'd never write about shipwrecks again, but this particular one got into my imagination and wouldn't let go. I am grateful to my children, Ben and Quinn, who asked me many times to tell them this tale on long car trips, and reminded me that a good Great Lakes yarn is hard to beat.

The book would not have been written without the generosity of the Georgian Bay Land Trust's King Family Bursary, Ontario Arts Council Writers' Reserve program and the extraordinary support of Lake Huron–born arts benefactor Richard Rooney. I am deeply thankful for Richard's support and commitment to creating new works.

I am also incredibly lucky to have smart friends who generously read my earliest drafts, including Rosemary Renton, who is a creative genius and has been my muse since high school, and filmmaker/director/hockey inspiration Chris Deacon, who also enlisted her daughter Callie Deacon and niece Tashi Gombu to offer their smarts and insight. Over the last seven years, the kids at Word-Play: Writing in the City (www.word-play.ca) have motivated me each week with their creativity, intelligence, love of books and willingness to participate in all the silly games I make up. I wrote this book in the hope that it might be something they will want to read.

My agent, Jackie Kaiser, has had my back from the beginning, and I am so grateful for her wise counsel and willingness to fight for me and my work these many moons. I'm also delighted to be working with the good people at Orca Book Publishers. Thank you to Ruth Linka and Andrew Wooldridge for their early enthusiasm, to copyeditor Vivian Sinclair and sensitivity reader Greg Younging, as well as designer Rachel Page, illustrator Jacqui Oakley and Orca marketing coordinator Jen Cameron. Special thanks to Tanya Trafford, editor extraordinaire, who asks all the right questions.

Finally, I am forever grateful to my parents, Jim and Erica Curtis, who have always encouraged my writing and fostered my passion for Georgian Bay, and to Nick, whose love makes all things possible.

ANDREA CURTIS is the award-winning writer of several books for young people and adults, including *Into the Blue*, the story of her great-grandfather, a steamboat captain who disappeared on Georgian Bay in the early twentieth century. Andrea lives in Toronto, Ontario, with her husband and their two sons. *Big Water* is her first novel. For more information, visit www.andreacurtiskids.ca.